COLLECT CALL
to MY MOTHER

LORI HORVITZ

COLLECT CALL *to* MY MOTHER
ESSAYS ON LOVE, GRIEF, AND GETTING A GOOD NIGHT'S SLEEP

COPYRIGHT © 2023 by Lori Horvitz
COVER PHOTO: "Lori H, 1982," courtesy of Lisa Perrott
COVER AND BOOK DESIGN by Alexandru Oprescu

All rights reserved. Published by New Meridian, part of the non-profit organization New Meridian Arts, 2023.

No part of this publication may be reproduced, or stored in a retrieval system, or transmitted in any form or by any means, electronic, mechanical, photocopying, or otherwise, without written permission of the publisher, except in the case of brief quotations in reviews. For information regarding permission, write to newmeridianarts1@gmail.com

LIBRARY OF CONGRESS CATALOGING-IN-PUBLICATION DATA

Collect Call to My Mother: Essays on Love, Grief, and Getting a Good Night's Sleep
Authored by Lori Horvitz

ISBN: 9798985965926
LCCN: 2022943876

AUTHOR'S NOTE: This is a work of creative nonfiction. While all the stories in this book are true to the best of my recollection, most names and identifying characteristics have been changed to protect the privacy of those involved. I recreated scenes and dialogue in a way to evoke the story's essence—based on journals, emails, interviews, and memory. And we all know, depending on one's perspective, there's a certain lawlessness to memory.

ACKNOWLEDGMENTS

I WOULD LIKE TO THANK the many friends and writers who provided encouragement and generous feedback on my manuscript. For the gift of time and space, I am grateful to the Ragdale Foundation, Brush Creek Foundation for the Arts, Vermont Studio Center, and Virginia Center for the Creative Arts. For believing in and publishing my book, I'm indebted to New Meridian Arts Literary Press. To my students, friends, and community in Asheville, I offer you my gratitude. And most of all, thank you Kristen Dotti, for believing in me before I believed in myself.

Excerpts or chapters of this book have first appeared, often in different forms, in *The Laurel Review*, *Under the Sun*, *North Dakota Quarterly*, *Hobart*, *The MacGuffin*, *Entropy*, *South 85 Journal*, *AMP*, *The Hunger*, *decomp journal*, *Cumberland River Review*, *South Dakota Review*, *Dash*, *Redivider*, and *Chattahoochee Review*.

CONTENTS

COLLECT CALL *to* MY MOTHER.......................... 1
A GIRL'S GUIDE *to* HOT MESS YOGA 7
MAKING CONTACT..................................... 17
DAYTONA BEACH, 1950 21
ALL *the* WORLD'S OCEANS 27
THE GIFT-GIVER...................................... 31
THE ISLAND *of* TSK 41
COOL *as* PATTY HEARST 47
THOSE FRIDAY AFTERNOONS.......................... 51
THE MICROWAVE 57
GIRL *in the* MAROON VELVET GOWN 59
A THREESOME *with* TIME 61
MY FATHER'S MUG 69
ON DEATH *and* DYING (MY HAIR)....................... 73
SLEEP CYCLES 77
THE GRIEF BIRD 83
ON *the* BENEFITS *of* LIQUID SOAP 87
CHASING SQUIRRELS.................................. 95
THE SCENT *of* NAG CHAMPA 101
THREE VETERINARIANS............................... 109
HOLDING SPACE...................................... 115
BIG GUTS / BIG HEARTS 119
DRESS UP *as a* LITERARY FIGURE 127
THE LAST FREIGHT TRAIN 135
MY HISTORY *of* WAITING 143
LESBIAN CINDERELLA 149
THE END *of* AIR HUGS................................. 153
SEARCH *and* RESCUE 157
THE SECRET LIFE *of* VOLES 163
COMFORTABLE SHOES 171
ONE WITHERING ROSE................................ 179
THE STORY *of a* MIRROR 185
I REMEMBER YOU, ALLEN GINSBERG.................... 189
VICTORY LAP... 197
UNLIMITED MINUTES 207

for Kristen

COLLECT CALL *to* MY MOTHER

I T WAS CHEAPER TO TAKE A NIGHT TRAIN to Oslo than pay for a hotel, and on the train from Frankfurt, I met a soft-spoken blonde guy, the kind of guy who majors in business and takes up golf, who rows for his college crew team, who eventually takes over his father's business. The kind of guy I'd never typically meet, let alone spend hours sharing stories with at two in the morning. He had just graduated from college and his parents gave him a wad of money to backpack around Europe, and I'd been out of college for a year and saved up money from creating corporate slide presentations at a god-awful advertising agency, and there we were, the Manhattan hippie chick and the blonde golf guy sitting together, nodding off together, laughing with the Finnish man sharing our compartment, even though we had little clue what he was talking about. With our giant backpacks, we made our way to the Oslo Youth Hostel, dropped our packs off and searched for food. We passed a post office, where one could make international calls, way before the days of cell phones and email, and Golf Guy said he wanted to call his parents and I said, what the hell, I'd try to call my parents too, and we wrote down our numbers and gave them to the clerk and walked into booths and I held the receiver and my mother picked up. The operator asked if she'd accept my collect call.

"No," my mother said.

I sat in the booth for a couple minutes, a little stunned.

My mother said no. Then again what did I expect? I knew my mother was stingy—after all, at McDonald's, she'd only get four bags of French fries and divide them among the six in our family. Of course she didn't want to spend the few dollars per minute it would cost to accept the call.

I walked by Golf Guy's booth and he was laughing, his raised foot resting against the wall in front of him.

I told him my parents weren't home.

It's not like I ever attempted to make a collect call before, not if you don't count the times I called from Penn Station, on my way to visit my parents on Long Island, and the operator would say, "Collect call…" and before they could answer, I'd say, "I'm coming in on the 3:04 train!" and hang up.

Now my mother said no. Years later, I took a financial literacy class for women. The instructor asked how we learned about money, what our emotional relationship with it looks like, and I remembered my mother not accepting that call. In groups of three, we shared our experiences. One woman in my group began to sob. "My father," she said, "left my mother when I was two. She only had a high school degree and had to support two small children. She cleaned houses. Some days we went hungry."

Another woman in the group put her hand on the crying woman's arm.

I told the group about my mother not accepting my call because she didn't want to spend the money. "What kind of mother," I said, "doesn't accept a collect call from her twenty-one year-old daughter who she knew was traveling alone in Europe without an itinerary?"

The crying woman snapped her head up, brushed strands of hair from her face. "I gotta say," she said, "that's just sad."

"I could have been raped or kidnapped or robbed. I could have been in an accident and broken my leg." I tried to hold back from crying. "I could have really needed my mother."

While she yapped away on a turquoise rotary phone, my mother drew pages of doodles, her one creative outlet. As a college student, she studied drawing, painting, and fashion design, but after marriage, she abandoned her creative endeavors. I took up visual arts in college—photography and printmaking—but when I gave her a silkscreen print, she said, "I would have liked gold hoop earrings instead."

I try to imagine what my mother did after she got off the phone with the Norwegian operator. Maybe she went antique shopping, or maybe she hummed to herself while searching for shoes at Roosevelt Field Mall, or maybe she went to Frederick's Beauty School, where she stared at her freckled face in the mirror and made sure her hair color was red but not too red. Did she think at any point that maybe she should have accepted my call?

It's not like she couldn't afford to accept the call—my parents were schoolteachers. Besides, we weren't the "keep in touch and call me when you get there" type of family.

I continued to step on and off trains. I traveled with Golf Guy up to Narvik, where golds and reds and oranges lit up the sky, where we played Frisbee under the Midnight Sun. I traveled to a dusty gray town in Finland and stayed in a youth hostel, where the only other person in my room full of bunk beds was an older German woman who talked to herself and wore glasses with no glass in them.

Traveling to Europe was a sure way to get distance from my boyfriend of two years, the charming intellect who looked like John Lennon and called himself an anarchist. Every once in a while, he'd rage at me and call me a cheap Jew, yelling that all museums should be smashed and made into community centers for "The People." After I graduated college, we sublet a room in New York City but he left a month later and went home to Syracuse, claiming he hated the city and corporate Yuppie scum. Two months later, we moved into a gas-smelling apartment on a slant, just north of Manhattan. But he left me again to finish his degree. I found an apartment share in Hell's Kitchen, by the Theatre District, with an aspiring cross-eyed actress named Twyla and saved money to travel. The boyfriend now wanted to move to Minneapolis, where he said we could start a new life, where his best buddy just moved to attend graduate school and claimed that Minneapolis was full of jobs and anarchists.

I told the boyfriend I was going to Europe and didn't know how long I'd be there.

But after my mother said no, after feeling sad and lonely in Scandinavia, I made a collect call to the boyfriend. He accepted. He told me he loved me and missed me and I said yes. I wanted to go with him to Minneapolis.

This is how it started. My mother said no, and the boyfriend said yes.

I flew back to New York and phoned my parents from Kennedy Airport. No one answered. Since I had no where else to go, I took the Long Island Railroad to my hometown and walked into my house and no one was there, not even the dog, but her water bowl, filled to the brim, was under the table. I called my brother, who lived with a friend in the next town, and he said my parents went to Cape Cod and the poodle died of a heart attack in her sleep.

The boyfriend said his buddy in Minneapolis would pay for a rental truck if he hauled the friend's furniture, and a week later, the boyfriend drove a truck from Upstate New York and parked it in front of my childhood home and we loaded my stuff. My mother stared straight ahead and my father said, "You'll be back in a month." The truck broke down in Harlem and we spent hours waiting for a mechanic to fix it. Once we got on the road, the headlights didn't work. We slept in the back of the truck in a hotel parking lot because the hotel was booked up and we couldn't drive in the dark.

Minneapolis was not full of anarchists and jobs. After a month we packed up my futon and sent it with us on a Greyhound bus, both of us thrilled to be back in New York, where I found an apartment in Alphabet City, an apartment that had its kitchen window shattered; the prior tenant moved out after a thief broke in from the abandoned building next door and took all his valuables and walked out the front door. But now it was our place, including roaches, mice, and bars drilled into every window.

I never told my parents I lived with the boyfriend—we never talked about anything personal—and if he answered when my mother called, he handed me the phone. She never asked why a man had answered the phone.

Something happened to my mother between her college days, when according to an uncle, she created art and was full of life, and her childrearing days. Maybe the pressure to marry and have children—she had four children in five years—overwhelmed her. As a single child of Russian immigrants, a child growing up during the Great Depression, perhaps my mother felt lonely and scared; this might be the reason she found solace in hoarding junk and taking control of money in odd ways.

I don't remember my mother ever hugging me, or reading me a book, or even listening, really listening to me. But in my sophomore year of college, I remember sitting with her in our yard. I told her how upset I was about a boy who had just broken my heart. I can't remember what she said, but I do remember her saying her family was the most important part of her life. I believe she meant it. But something blocked her from acting on it.

I don't have children, but if I did, I hope I'd have the emotional capacity to nurture my child, to read to her, to hold her when she needed holding, to answer the phone when she called. When my dog goes to the groomer I miss her. The house feels empty. And as I write this, I'm away from home, and yesterday my dog sitter put the receiver to my dog's ear and I called her name and my dog cocked her head and licked the phone.

Maybe this is one reason why I traveled so much in my twenties; on the road, I didn't have to think about my family, or missing them, or if they thought about me. I could wander and make new friends, as if they were family, like the sweet Golf Guy. And maybe this is why I'd never consider Golf Guy as boyfriend material and instead pined away for a moody anarchist.

It's over thirty years later and my mother's been dead for a good portion of that time. Four years after she said no to my collect call, a car accident took her life. I was traveling in Italy and didn't learn of her death until the day of the funeral. I am now the same age she'd been when I called home but she wouldn't accept the call.

"All the money in the world," I told my therapist, "couldn't pay for a one-minute conversation with my mother."

"What would you say," she said, "if you could talk to her?"

"We could have traveled together," I said. "Just us. And eaten all the damn French fries we wanted."

That night, I dreamt I entered the back door of my childhood home and walked up the stairs. My mother stood at the landing and hugged me. I said, "This is a dream, isn't it?" She kept hugging me. I said, "It's a dream, right?" She continued to embrace me. I woke up crying.

A GIRL'S GUIDE *to* HOT MESS YOGA

IMAGINE LYING IN BED, drifting off to sleep, when you receive a text from a model-slinky Natalie Portman look-a-like. She says *I can't stop thinking about you, I can't wait to kiss you,* and her texts get more suggestive. You never sexted before, but find yourself sexting, and now you're not so tired. This Natalie Portman woman is named, coincidentally, Natalie. You met her two weeks before, at a bookstore, at your reading, and you went for coffee. She smiled a lot, whipped her hair back, applied gloss to her lips. She told you about her love of animals, her work as a veterinarian, how her favorite surgery to perform was bladder surgery because the bladder is so elastic. Charmed by her smarts, her gentle voice, a voice that could calm the anxious owner of a sick poodle, you exchanged phone numbers, figuring that was that. You didn't expect anything more than a Facebook friend request. After all, she lived a plane ride away and had three young children. But the next day she texted, said she was smitten, and you said, well, come visit, figuring she wouldn't.

You talk on Skype, her three-year old daughter in her lap, touching her face. She asks if you're dating anyone. You say you haven't been with anyone in eight months. She asks how you manage. You say, "How do you think?" She tells you she's dating two people—a man, a woman, nothing serious, friends with benefits. "But you," she says. "You make my heart flutter." She hasn't felt this way since meeting her ex-husband. She bites her lip. You see yourself smiling in the corner of your computer screen. Behind Natalie, her son smacks her older daughter and her daughter screams. Natalie has to go, but before ending the call, she says she'd love to visit.

She texts details of a proposed flight, and your anxiety level shoots up, and your heart races and your gut hurts. You run to a yoga class and breathe and can't find your center, even when resting in *shavasana* position. You write Natalie an email, ask how this is going to work, with her three children, and living across the country, and seeing other people. After all, you're looking for a long-term relationship. She says maybe down the line she'd be ready for monogamy, but she just left an abusive marriage, she needs time, she wishes she met you in a year. But if you only want a friendship, she says, that's fine too.

You Skype, and as soon as you see her face, her lips, as soon as she says, "It's okay, I understand why you'd be concerned," you cut her off and say, "Yes, I'd love for you to visit."

You've always been monogamous, except for a year or two, after you got involved with a British woman, the first woman you'd been with, the woman you met on a slow-train to China, when you were twenty-three. She talked about monogamy, how it was so bloody boring, and you thought, yeah, you're right, it's so bloody boring. When you came back to the States, your moody ex-boyfriend promised he'd change and wanted to try again, and you said okay, only if you could date others. You dated a boyishly handsome Englishman and had a fling with a blonde Catholic girl, and there were others. And for a moment you thought you were so fucking hip. But in the end, your heart couldn't take it, and when New Year's Eve came around, you told them all you were sick and stayed home because it was easier that way.

Natalie tells you about the psychological test she took in order to gain custody of her children, how it came out fine except for one thing; something that could be construed as negative—she has hedonist tendencies. You say, "What's wrong with wanting pleasure?"

Before she visits, you ask what foods she likes. She says she loves cake, especially chocolate cake, and you say you love a good chocolate cake too. She loves making cake, and at that moment, she's making a dragon cake for her daughter's birthday. She sends you a picture, and you ask how she made the dragon's scales. "It's fondant," she says. "What fancy wedding cakes are covered in. Making cakes is my one kitschy secret."

You meet in the airport, and all the sexting makes things awkward, so you keep your distance, don't make eye contact. In the car she comments about the beautiful mountains in the distance, applies lip-gloss. Once you arrive to your house, she gets down on the kitchen floor and scratches behind your dog's ears. You ask if she could check the lumps on your dog's belly; after all, Natalie works as a veterinarian. She palpates the pup's abdomen, says you shouldn't worry. Natalie's roller suitcase stands upright, and she wheels it behind you as you lead her to the guestroom, no assumptions.

You take her to an Indian restaurant and eat fried onion dumplings and dip them in tamarind sauce, which you refer to as magic sauce. Natalie's foot touches yours and you freeze, then move your foot closer. She leans her elbows on the table, her silver bracelets clanking downward. She thanks you for inviting her.

Later, you lie down on your bed and ask if she wants to join you. She rests her body near yours and asks if you'll kiss her, and you do, and you don't think about her kids or friends with benefits, and the kiss lasts and lasts, and you can't keep our hands off each other, even when walking through the Blue Ridge Mountains, and you watch the sun go down and feel a calmness you haven't felt before.

Everyone who meets Natalie—the lesbian waitress at the local cafe, the colleagues you run into at the farmer's market, the friend you meet up with at the sushi restaurant—comments how Natalie is hot, a looker, and you say she is also sweet and smart, and a doctor, and now you're confident and goofy, and when the magical weekend comes to an end, you bring her to the airport and take selfies of her kissing your cheek, a big grin on your face. She asks when you'll visit and you say soon.

Now she only has time for the occasional text, too busy with the kids, the lawyers, the job, even at night, and you don't think she's still sleeping with the others, why would she when she has you? Or maybe you don't want to know. Natalie sends a text: *Being with you makes me feel beautiful, like I have no flaws.* You buy a plane ticket.

Sweat coats your body at night and granted, menopause has kicked in, and even though Natalie texts now and again, you get sweaty and anxious and run to yoga. You've never gone to so many yoga classes. In the past, yoga made you anxious. You could never follow directions, and the teachers tugged and pushed at your body to help you get in the correct position, which only made you more anxious, but now, thank heavens, yoga calms you.

You ask Natalie if she still sleeps with her friends with benefits, and she says yes, she still sees them, though it's only sex. She knows most people can't understand, but after spending so many years in a controlling relationship, she's not ready for monogamy. "Down the line," she says, "I could get there." But her heart is opening, and her kids can't wait to meet you, and she'll make you her delicious chocolate cake.

Natalie's explanation, in theory, makes perfect sense, so you try to be understanding and empathetic. After all, you're a women's studies professor, and besides, you've already bought the plane ticket, and as a consolation prize, you'll have good sex and homemade chocolate cake.

When you step into Natalie's arms, your anxiety falls away. In her white minivan, three empty child safety seats in the back, you kiss and grope and you move Natalie's hair from her face, and things get sweaty and hot and you say, "Let's not get caught making out in the airport parking lot." She drives to a pub and you hold hands and share a grilled salmon dish with ginger, your legs intertwined, and she tells you she's in no rush to get home, she hired a babysitter, and also, she spent the afternoon making chocolate cake. When the waitress asks if you're interested in dessert, you say we'll get that at home, meaning the cake, but the waitress rolls her eyes and walks away.

Natalie's children hold your hand and touch your face, and her daughter sits in your lap and wraps her arms around your waist. Natalie hands you a giant slice of cake, a slice so delicious, rich, moist and sweet you only eat a few bites.

Finally, finally, she tucks her children in, sings them lullabies, and crawls into bed with you, and you spend hours caressing her body, breathe it in as if it were your own breath. Now you don't miss yoga, you have Natalie, and you sleep well, so well you don't hear her get up and turn the television on downstairs. Even though she says she hates when her kids watch television, she lets them watch today, a special day because of you.

Natalie hires sitters to watch the children much of the weekend, but you do spend time building Lego cities and reading children's books, one after the next, and you show her younger daughter a magic trick. You point to a napkin covering a ball and raise your hands over the napkin and say "Abracadabra!" Then you slap the napkin down. Then you pull the ball from her ear, and she laughs and screams and says, "Do it again!" and you do, again and again, pulling the ball from her butt, her nose. You show her how to do the trick, how to make the ball's indentation by pressing down on the ball with napkins, and when you take the ball away, it looks like the ball is still there. You say, "It's an illusion. You believe the ball's there because it looks like it's there."

Natalie books a room at a five-star hotel overlooking a river, just the two of you and a king-sized bed. At the hotel restaurant, you eat homemade guacamole and fried oysters and don't think about breathing, not until late into the night, when you hold her and ask why she still sleeps with others. She says, "Because I like sex and you're not here." You look at the river and imagine another naked body lying near Natalie's. "If you get to the point where it's too hard for you," she says, "let me know."

You don't feel comfortable asking for that; you don't want to come off as possessive. The others are just sex, friends with benefits. You wrap your body around hers, and in the morning, she takes you to a hipster café, lots of tattoos and piercings, and she puts her arm around your shoulder. You eat scallion pancakes and eggs, and before she takes you to the airport, she tells her babysitter, a family friend, what's going on. "She was surprised," Natalie says, "but said she'd never seen me look so happy."

When you get back home, hot flashes and anxiety come back with a vengeance, and you inhale, exhale, take one yoga class after the next, but your lungs get tighter, your breath disappears like the ball underneath the napkin. One night, you guess she is with her male friend when she doesn't answer your texts, and you can't sleep, and now you don't care how well she treats your dog, how much she looks like a movie star, how great the sex is, because if you can't breathe, you can't live.

You tell her you understand she needs to do what she needs to do, but you need to take care of your heart. She had guessed how you were feeling, even discussed it with her male friend, but she doesn't want to lose you, and if she stops sleeping with the others, would you still see her, would you be her girlfriend?

Exhausted and weak, you say yes, you'll be her girlfriend.

Natalie makes time to talk every night, after she puts her kids to sleep, but sometimes it gets late, close to midnight, and you text *Maybe we could talk tomorrow,* and she says *Give me five minutes,* and you hate waiting, always waiting, especially when you need to teach in the morning. Fifteen or twenty minutes later, she calls, and for the moment, her voice soothes you.

When she visits again, she makes French toast and strawberries and real whipped cream and puts cream on her lips and you kiss. You walk through town, hand in hand, and you introduce Natalie to a friend you run into. Your friend later says Natalie is dreamy, that she could feel the energy between the two of you.

Maybe Natalie's the one, you think, maybe you could help raise her kids; you always wanted a family. She says, "It's so easy with you," and you say, "Yes, it's so easy," and she says her kids adore you, and you make plans to meet up in New York, your old stomping ground, a city she's never been to. You go shopping at Target for clothes, and in the fitting room you kiss, take selfies in the mirror, the two of you embracing in your new dresses.

In New York, you see the musical *Fun Home*, a coming out story of a young woman with an emotionally abusive father. During a particularly harsh scene, you hold Natalie's arm, scared she might be reminded of her abusive ex. Later she says it did rattle her but not so bad. You eat cannolis in Little Italy, and you take her to your favorite Cuban restaurant, where you meet your friend, who later says, "I like her best of all."

In the meantime, she goes out with her friends with benefits, without the benefits. You don't want to sound controlling, but you say it makes you feel uneasy. She says you shouldn't worry; she isn't even attracted to the guy. "Sex with you," she says, "is so much more fun." She has plans to go to a movie with him that evening. She asks if you want to FaceTime with him later. "Maybe," she says, "if you meet him it would ease your worries."

"I don't think so," you say, scanning the yoga schedule.

A week later, Natalie asks if you're sure you couldn't open up the relationship. Just the fact she asks makes you anxious. She dreams about you checking her phone—that's what her ex did, and again she asks about seeing other people and now you have to push your heart back into your chest.

You step into Natalie's mini-van and her son orders her to change the radio station, the other two children strapped in and silent. At a restaurant, a carousel in front, her kids jump on, and the antique horses move up and down, and carnival music blares, and around and around they go, until her kids are dizzy. Natalie takes pictures of her children waving. You make small talk, and because she doesn't make eye contact, you feel her vanishing. During the night, each child wakes up, one by one, screaming from nightmares, night terrors, wailing, and at six in the morning, alone in her bed, you get up to scan the rooms but can't find Natalie. Did she drive off and leave you with the kids? Do you have to call child protective services? You look again and find her sleeping beside her little girl, Natalie's body blocked by the bed railing.

She sorts through a box of her ex's stuff, to see if you want anything to sell at a garage sale to raise money for your sick friend. She pulls out beer mugs and a pair of army boots and slouches against the wall, face in hands, tears streaming from her eyes. "What's wrong?" you ask. She says, "Those boots; he kicked me with those boots."

Her son screams and rips up his underwear—he doesn't want to be confined by anything. And neither does Natalie. You sit her down. "You're disappearing," you say, "and so am I."

She tells you that last night she had come up with an escape plan. You say, "From me?"

"That's what I did with my ex," she says. "It has nothing to do with you." She cries and holds you, and you focus on an upside down doll, its legs sticking from one of the many unpacked boxes scattered around the house.

You change your flight to leave a day early. When her son learns you're leaving, he screams, asks why you have to go, why can't you marry his mother?

At the airport, you listen to announcements and watch businessmen and hipsters and mothers with children board planes. You are free of Lego pieces and screams in the night, relieved when you finally find your airplane seat. You can't wait to get home, to your dog, your friends, your self.

The pilot says something about a mechanical difficulty, it will be taken care of shortly, to hold tight. A mechanic who looks about twelve sprints to the back and everyone claps. Twenty minutes later, he walks through the cabin, his face sullen. Another mechanic climbs aboard. The sun goes down, and the new mechanic, after working for a good thirty minutes, walks to the front of the plane, his arms hanging down. "Folks," the pilot says. "We have bad news."

Four hours pass since Natalie dropped you off. You could get a hotel, but you text her. She asks if you want to come back. You say yes.

You call your dog-sitter. "Now that I've had some time and space," you say, "I'm ready to go back to Natalie's."

"It must have been really bad," your dog-sitter says, "for you to be ready to go back only after plane-ing and deplane-ing."

Natalie's son screams when you swing open the minivan door: "Yay! The plane broke! Maybe it'll break tomorrow too!"

You say, "Yay for the broken plane!"

Natalie touches your arm. She winks and says, "I'm glad the plane broke too."

You help Natalie prepare dinner, and when she drains pasta, you embrace her from behind. She leans her head back into yours and you kiss her neck. Her children don't notice, or care, but instead watch a video, Taylor Swift's "Shake it Off." Her younger daughter practices the vanishing ball trick and performs it for her brother. With his arms crossed, the boy analyzes his sister's every move. When she slaps the napkin, he jumps up and down and yells, "I know how you do it! I know!"

The ball falls to the floor and her son picks it up and screams for his other sister to watch while he performs the trick. "Abracadabra," he says, and pounds the napkin with his fist. He runs into the living room, where he shows her how the trick is done. "The ball was never there!" he says.

But for now, Natalie *is* there, free from commitment, free from confines, free from the future, and together, you find yourself breathless, alive, and wake up holding Natalie—no strings, no illusions, free of worry, free of waiting, your breath intact. Imagine that.

MAKING CONTACT

I'LL NEVER KNOW WHY JANET WELLINGTON, a fellow graduate student, looked down at her shoes when she passed me in the English Department hallway. We never argued, never took the same class, never even had a one-on-one conversation. During orientation, new students introduced themselves, and Janet, who had short red hair, pasty skin and a small turned-up nose, blinked a few times before telling us she grew up on a farm in Michigan, the working-class daughter of a dairy farmer.

It's not like she looked at her shoes when others passed. Just to prove it, I walked through the hallway with a friend, until Janet walked towards us. She said hi to my friend but stared down at her Doc Martens instead of acknowledging me. My friend laughed, said, "Oh my gosh! She really does look at her shoes when she passes you!" Although I laughed too, it bothered me, made me feel invisible. A feeling so familiar.

In junior high and high school, I never raised my hand, never said a word in class, not if I didn't have to. I walked through halls as if I were a ghost, floating from one class to the next, sitting alone at lunch, staring at the ticking clock, waiting for that last bell to ring. Teachers ignored me, but one day, my eighth grade algebra teacher called my name when I nodded off and yelled, "Wake up!"

I spent most of my childhood in my hot pink bedroom, alone, every so often staring in the mirror, until my eyes watered, until I saw a spooky medusa face. When I blinked I came back to myself—a shy, long-faced teenager with a mouthful of braces. I recorded myself, pretending to be a famous person interviewed by a talk-show host. Maybe this is why I took up photography and often set the self-timer and ran in front of the camera. I needed to see myself, hear myself, acknowledge myself.

"Why do you think," my therapist said, "Janet's behavior affects you to that extent?"
"She makes me feel invisible," I said.
"But you're not invisible," she said. "It's not about you."
"How is it *not* about me?" I said, waving my hands.
"Janet doesn't know you," she said. "Perhaps you represent something she's threatened by. It doesn't even matter. Your reaction is what matters. You're giving her power."

Two years into graduate school, the pattern with Janet continued. I had to do something, so I forced out a "hello" when we passed in the hallway. She'd lift her head marginally, still not making eye contact, but looked in my direction, grumbled a hello, and stared back at her shoes. If this were a power struggle, maybe I made headway.

A friend speculated Janet had a crush on me. Why else would she not make eye contact? Even though she wore khakis and white button-down shirts and could pass for an angry nun, or at least a serious academic lesbian, she often mentioned her heterosexual status. "Janet doesn't have a problem," my friend said, "appropriating lesbian attire, does she?"

One evening I threw a party for grad school friends and made sure to invite a new student, Tim—a frail, curly-haired guy who wore thick glasses and mumbled. I didn't invite Janet, not out of spite, but because she never made the effort to look at me. Nonetheless, she showed up, put two Heinekens in my refrigerator, as if she belonged in my house. She talked and laughed with Tim, all the while combing fingers through her hair. They soon began to date.

During our last year of grad school, Janet and I had to share an office.

Now was my chance to probe why she refused to acknowledge me. But I didn't know how or when to ask. Like two cats living in the same house but ignoring each other, for a full semester, we sat back to back, our desks facing opposite walls, where we met students and never exchanged a word.

Not until June, the last time I saw her. We found ourselves sharing a lane in the YMCA pool, standing side by side, taking a break. Maybe there was something about the water that made it impossible to look down. She took off her goggles and focused on my shoulder. "Did you know," she said, "it takes two weeks to get an appointment at Planned Parenthood?"

"Really?" I said, not sure why she was telling me this.

She made eye contact. "That's a long time, isn't it?"

"Maybe you can go somewhere else," I said, "if you need to see a doctor sooner."

"Two weeks is a long time, isn't it?" she said. She put her goggles on and disappeared under the water.

Did she only want to tell me about her need for birth control, that she was having sex?

Maybe it's okay not to know.

What I do know: Janet Wellington made eye contact with me in the YMCA pool. I also never had a chance to look my mother in the eye and say goodbye.

Now I slunk my body back into the pool and swam a few feet behind Janet Wellington, her bare feet kicking up and down, splashing me in the face, so I slowed down and let her pull two body lengths ahead.

DAYTONA BEACH, 1950

In the living room of my grandparents' Brighton Beach high-rise, the Coney Island skyline in the horizon, I leapt and twirled and performed unrehearsed pirouettes, while Aunt Irene, my only unmarried adult relative, clapped and stomped her foot. At the conclusion of "Sunrise, Sunset," I bowed. My parents, siblings and other relatives limply clapped, but Aunt Irene, her red lipstick smile taking up half her face, whistled and hugged my seven-year old body. Not used to getting this kind of attention, I didn't know what to do but cry. Tears streamed down my face, leading to a full heaving weep. My grandma handed me tissues and asked what was wrong, my grandfather told her to leave me alone, and Aunt Irene rubbed my back and told me how talented I was.

A year later, Aunt Irene died of Raynaud's disease—a debilitating autoimmune disorder. After the funeral, relatives looted her Long Island City apartment, full of souvenirs from Russia, Cuba, South America. My mother picked out a balalaika from Moscow and two serapes from Mexico. Uncle Joe, Aunt Irene's brother, said, "She was a beauty. So many men proposed to her. No one was good enough."

"And look what happened," Grandma Becky said. As if Aunt Irene's single life brought on an early demise and the pilfering of her possessions.

No man was good enough because I'm pretty sure Aunt Irene was a lesbian.

She traveled the world and wore a permanent smile, unlike her morose older sister, Grandma Becky—who shuffled her legs, every step a hardship, as if just disembarking from a Russian steamer; fifty years before, both had stepped onto North American soil for the first time. Their family had settled into a boarding house in Montreal, where sixteen-year old Becky met a young tailor named Harry. They had a brief romance, before his family moved to Brooklyn. Three years later, when Becky's family moved to Brooklyn and the couple reunited, she no longer felt the same passion. But she married him because, she told me a few years before her death, "He bought me a ring."

Soon after Grandma Becky passed (Aunt Irene had been dead for twenty years), I inherited a box of Aunt Irene's photos, including a picture of my aunt, arm in arm with another woman in front of a big ol' Chevy, written on the back: *Daytona Beach, 1950*. Both women were feminine and Katharine-Hepburn pretty—an image that would imprint on my brain, deep as the comment made by Uncle Joe. Although I had suspicions about my aunt's sexuality, now I had evidence.

Unlike other relatives, my aunt exuded a thirst for life. Although I tried to channel that positivity, at the time I found the photo, it wasn't possible. My girlfriend of three and half years had just broken up with me. I couldn't blame her. I had refused to come out and wouldn't go to therapy. I wouldn't even hold her hand in public. "We'll get gay-bashed," I had told her. In truth I felt shame for being with a woman. My internalized homophobia and self-loathing overpowered the reality that Aunt Irene might have been a happy lesbian. Holding onto an ancestral glimmer of hope through Aunt Irene hadn't occurred to me.

Now I tried to convince myself that at twenty-eight, I needed to meet the right man and settle down. A friend and I placed personal ads in the *New York Press*, a free weekly paper. At least we'd have each other to compare notes. My ad started out: *SWF, 28, seeks creative male who hates television.* My friend's ad: *SWF, seeks male who loves television.* We had to call into a voicemail number to retrieve our messages. I met up with one man—a filmmaker who said, "I hate television too. We have a lot not to talk about." We chatted for hours at a small café, but I felt nothing. Was this how Grandma Becky felt on her wedding day? Was this my choice? A passionless marriage with a decent guy?

Despite his anger and anti-Semitic quips, I had stayed with my college boyfriend for five years. This was love. At least the love I had known. A typical scenario from my childhood: following an argument between my parents, my mother sat on a turquoise kitchen chair, head in hands, and sobbed, while my father mentioned the $99 no-fault divorce advertised on the radio. I never saw affection displayed between my parents or grandparents, in contrast to the carefree, smiling Aunt Irene on the beach with her "friend."

Three years after arriving to Manhattan from Minneapolis, the boyfriend broke up with me and moved around the corner. As a cure for heartache, I sublet my apartment, traveled through Europe for five months, and met the British woman on the Trans-Siberian Railway. Like him, she claimed to be an anarchist. My world opened up, as if having corrective eye surgery. Before that time, I might as well have been walking in a daze, as if I were an emigrant stepping off the Russian steamer, not knowing the language or customs. Three days later, when I returned to home, the New York anarchist pleaded to get back together, apologized for his bad behavior and charmed me by spending hours cooking an Indian meal. I said only if I could see other people. He agreed. I came out as bisexual. "I always knew," he said, "you were a lesbian." His rationale: I wouldn't date him when he first asked me out during my freshman year.

He put up with me dating other people, including the British woman. One night, during her visit to New York, the three of us dined together. Since they were both self-proclaimed anarchists, the two had a lot to discuss. I didn't call myself an anarchist, yet I unwittingly practiced anarchy of the heart by being involved with a woman who had other lovers, by convincing myself that this was the cool thing to do. I would have never invited another man I had been dating. And my boyfriend never would have joined us. After all, he had a tendency to storm off if I merely ran into a male friend. By inviting him out with a woman I loved, how could I have taken my relationship with her seriously? Most likely, my boyfriend and I looked at the situation as an edgy curiosity; at least I had the pretense of this. In retrospect, not only did this cause me pain, I hurt others by lying to myself and denying what I truly wanted, which was what I saw, or at least imagined, in Aunt Irene's photo—two women who loved and supported each other without shame or obligation.

A year later, I cut off my relationship with the boyfriend and embarked on my first committed relationship with a woman—the girlfriend who broke up with me because I wouldn't come out. I didn't tell close friends, or lied and said I was still with the ex-boyfriend. Mostly I hated myself for lying, for feeling like I had to lie.

Despite the hypothetical resolve to find a man after the breakup with my first girlfriend, I frequented lesbian bars, sometimes with my straight guy friends. One night I met a woman who had just split up with her girlfriend of twenty years. In all that time, she told me, they had never mentioned the word "lesbian."

When I hid the most basic part of who I was, self-hatred ran deep. It made sense though, because what I learned about lesbians from the media—they were ugly, hairy man-haters who looked like men (or nuns). Not until I was in my late thirties did I feel comfortable enough to talk openly about my romantic life with friends. Prior to that, when my heart broke over and over, a piece of me felt like I deserved it, my punishment for liking girls, and I needed to suffer in silence. Yet I managed my shame by taking off to foreign countries every year, to distract myself, to explore new cultures, to wipe my identity slate clean. I wonder if Aunt Irene traveled for the same reasons. At home, however, she managed to be light and stomp her feet and smile.

After the breakup with my girlfriend, I traveled to Eastern Bloc countries, including Poland, where I visited Auschwitz. I learned about gay men imprisoned in concentration camps. Targeted for persecution, they were viewed as corrupting German values and didn't contribute to the growth of the "Aryan" population. Yet the Nazis weren't as concerned with lesbians: they could still mother as many babies as possible—a German woman's primary role. Some say the Nazis didn't persecute lesbians to the same degree because women in general were not seen as sexual beings.

Maybe my own internalized homophobia had been rooted in this notion. And if a woman took ownership of her sexuality, she'd be considered a whore, a slut, easy. What I've learned all my life—women need to be coupled with a man or else they'd be miserable and die alone.

In my mid-thirties, my father asked, "Don't you meet any men? Why don't you find a man and get married and get it over with?" Is that what he did? What Grandma Becky did?

"I meet lots of men," I said, and changed the subject.

In the 1940's and 50's, when Aunt Irene explored the world, few women traveled alone. Yet maybe Aunt Irene didn't travel solo. Maybe she traveled with the beautiful woman in the photo. Maybe she followed her heart as best as she could, given the times. Maybe she was happy because she didn't marry a man and live a "normal life," like many lesbians back then. I want to believe that the woman in the photo was her life partner, that she was able to live a happy life without compromise.

Before the beach photo was taken, I imagine the two women checking into the bottom floor of a dank Daytona Beach motel.

They're tired and excited after two long days of driving from Brooklyn. With motel key in hand, my aunt's partner parks the car in front of the room. Excited to feel the ocean breeze, they unload their bags, put on bathing suits and grab a couple towels from the bathroom. Before exiting, my aunt grabs her partner's hand and pulls her on the springy bed and they wrap their arms around each other and kiss. My aunt doesn't know her lipstick smears slightly, not until she gets to the beach, where her partner raises her finger delicately and rubs the mark off.

Maybe the joy Aunt Irene exuded and the perpetual smile on her face was genuine, the same grin she wore while I leapt across the blue carpet and performed pirouettes in my grandparents' twentieth floor high-rise. Perhaps she saw a glimmer of herself in me and gave me the encouragement she knew I wouldn't get otherwise. After I calmed down and wiped away my tears, she clapped and begged for another. "Brava!" she yelled. "One more!" Once again I twirled and jumped and beamed at Aunt Irene, the Coney Island parachute jump standing tall and proud in the distance.

ALL *the* WORLD'S OCEANS

MY MOTHER LOST HER INDEPENDENCE ON Independence Day, the day she married my father and moved from Brooklyn to southern Illinois, where he worked as a traveling salesman, leaving her isolated, surrounded by corn and wheat fields. Nothing much to do but give birth, four in a row, bam bam bam and me, the fourth, the grand finale, before my father got fired for "being too honest," before we all up and left, back to New York, to a landfill suburb, where I never saw a garlic clove, where pimentos grew in olives, where no one walked except a bald man in a trench coat, someone's weird uncle, and we all pointed at him because he walked. "Look at that man walking," we'd say. "He must be crazy."

My mother loved to travel, to escape, and my father reluctantly accompanied her. He talked about my mother in third person: "The woman is wild, always clomping like a horse. She can't sit still for a second." He documented their trips with an eight-millimeter movie camera, and after their Italy trip he showed us footage of Pompeii, the bodies embalmed in plaster white. A volcano erupts and bam bam bam, they're all dead. One witness on record said the dust "poured across the land like a flood…and shrouded the city in a darkness… like the black of closed and unlighted rooms," and now it was a museum, and I hadn't thought, not until visiting Pompeii myself, about how nature can be so exquisite, so useful, so loving, so cruel.

Sailors used landmarks such as glowing volcanoes to guide them—our first lighthouses, the traffic signs of the sea, our warning signals. The first lighthouse on record, Pharos Lighthouse, on the eastern point of Pharos Island in Egypt, used an open fire at the top as a source of light. Built about 280 BC, it was one of the Seven Wonders of the Ancient World and hence, people who study lighthouses are called Pharologists. In Pompeii, a nearby column of smoke, "like an umbrella pine," a clear warning sign of the impending explosion, triggered a response of curiosity rather than alarm, along with the many little earthquakes leading up to the big Vesuvius roar, and the volcanic explosion fifteen years prior was bad but reparable, so they repaired and repaired, hauled rocks and marble pillars for better days to come, but didn't think about the ruins I'd be walking through over two thousand years later.

Fifteen years after seeing my parents' Pompeii footage, I made my way to Pompeii and filmed plaster casts, a hand gripping a nearby foot, unfinished frescoes, petrified canines in corners, a group of women embalmed in a toga-draped, huddled embrace. That night, I returned to my Rome motel room and dreamt of black smoke spiraling from a burning car, a circle of Middle-Eastern boys chanting around it, precisely at the same time my mother died, but this was before the internet and cell phones, and I knew nothing about the crash or death for two days, not until after my mother was buried, underground, not unless you count my dream and I do.

My super-8 film shot at Pompeii came back from the lab and I ripped the package open but only blackness filled each frame, "like the black of a closed and unlighted room," exposed to too much light, or never exposed to any, I'll never know. Blinded by the light or kept in the dark, not much difference. The Russian meaning of my grandfather's last name is "blind man." By the time my grandfather reached Canada from the Ukraine, his name transformed from blind man to Blank. Harry Blank. Blank slate. Fill in the blank. My mother met my father on a blind date. No lights could break through the fog.

When a beam of light isn't visible from a lighthouse, when there's too much moisture in the air, an automatic sensor activates a foghorn. The first foghorn, used in 1719, was in the form of a cannon. The Boston lighthouse keeper fired a cannon every hour in the thick of the fog and no one got much sleep, and since my mother's death, I've suffered from insomnia, sometimes waking up every hour on the hour, even without the cannons.

I walked a lighthouse stairwell all the way to the top, and I heard a cannon's boom, but neither prepared me for my first glimpse of the Pacific—hungry and wild and out of control. At sixteen, in no way versed in trees or stars or birdcalls, I cried, overwhelmed by the ocean's cobalt waves, the craggy mountaintops, a cloud in the shape of a racing greyhound. I rode my bicycle towards those deep blues and purples and greens, tears running down my face, somewhere near Eureka, California, and later learned the word "Eureka" comes from the ancient Greek word meaning "I have found it," and I did find it, more beauty than I could imagine.

The rain of ash and pumice spewing from Mt. Vesuvius wasn't lethal at first, and the eruption, which lasted twenty-four hours, wasn't blinding at first, so those who fled immediately had a chance to survive, yet those who went back for possessions didn't have a chance. Scientists believe the fourth Vesuvius surge caused most of the fatalities, when a blanket of scolding ashy air, over five hundred degrees Fahrenheit, covered Pompeii, instantly incinerating bodies, and afterward, a larger deposit of ash buried them, leaving perfect body casts, frozen in time, some clutching jewelry and money, hands curled around gold coins as if they could use them as collateral in their next life.

Harry Blank and his future wife, Becky, were amongst those who saw the warning signs in Russia and had a chance for a new life, when a systematic policy of discrimination towards Jews led to their mass exodus in the early twentieth century. They moved from the Ukraine cornfields to a Montreal boarding house to a Brooklyn tenement to a Brighton Beach high-rise.

I never understood the ocean's fury, not as a child, and even as an adult, I could barely fathom how the Indian Ocean tsunami swallowed up entire towns, why foghorns didn't sound, why so many were taken by surprise. Beforehand, cows and dogs and other animals fled to higher ground and most survived, probably sensed ground vibrations. If the ground beneath your feet starts to move, get out of there as fast as you can. If there's a fire, stay low to the ground, but as a child, fires meant chasing after fire trucks on my banana-seat bicycle, and hurricanes meant sitting on a cot at the local armory, eating tuna sandwich triangles provided by the Red Cross and feeling disappointed when the meteorologist said it's safe, the eye of the storm has passed, go home.

My family moved from the Illinois cornfields to a split-level suburban house, a block from the Atlantic—our cross street: Bliss Place. Sometimes I found bliss: when I planted wheat seeds and watched them sprout; when my mother brought home three chickens from her kindergarten class and I claimed one for my own until I tried to kiss it and it poked me in the eye; when my mother gave me a seashell and I stroked its pearly orange inside and she told me to hold it up to my ear and I said why and she said you have to listen carefully and if you do you can hear the ocean and I pressed it against my ear and I said I can't hear anything and she said, listen, really listen, and I pressed the shell even harder and by gosh, the ocean roared in that shell, the shell that barely fit over my ear—a child with the ocean, all the world's oceans, in the palm of her hand.

THE GIFT-GIVER

I STOPPED BREATHING in a crowded Latin cuisine restaurant while on a date with a woman I'd known for twenty-four hours. Following the arrival of our main course, she had asked, "Is there something you've done that you're not proud of?" I told her about a rich woman I was involved with—she kept giving me gifts, and even though all the gift-giving made me anxious, even though I told her I had my own money, I accepted her offerings: an iPad on our first meeting, a MacBook Air on our second, and among other items, a 12-piece stainless steel cookware set. Maybe I took her gifts because on every birthday, my mother gave me a yellowed card from a stockpile of donated cards—she was the head of the rummage sale committee of two Jewish women's organizations—with a twenty-dollar bill inside. And on my thirteenth birthday, my mother bought me an unclaimed custom fitted and drilled bowling ball with a stranger's initials engraved into it.

I suppose a piece of me relished the iPad and other gifts, just like a part of me soaked up the attention the gift-giver lavished upon me. She said she didn't have motives; she was a generous person. She said I'd never have to feel alone again. She said my dead mother and her dead father orchestrated our meeting via OkCupid.

In the Latin cuisine restaurant, a piece of food lodged in my esophagus, so I gulped water to wash it down. But the water spewed up onto my almond-encrusted chicken, and I couldn't breathe, and my date asked if I was okay, and I mouthed NO and she got up and did the Heimlich maneuver, but I still couldn't breathe, and now all eyes focused on me, even the table of people across the way that just sang "Happy Birthday." The waitress asked if I was all right. My date said I wasn't. An older man, maybe a doctor, did the Heimlich maneuver, and I started talking. He said, "She's okay, she's talking," and walked back to his table. Whatever was lodged in my esophagus was still there and it hurt, but I could breathe, one breath in, one breath out. My date asked if I wanted to use the powder room, if I needed time alone. I wanted to remain seated, to make sure people were around if I lost my breath again. And besides, who calls the bathroom "a powder room"? My date took charge and paid the bill. Ten minutes later we left the restaurant. I said I shouldn't have talked about the woman who kept buying me gifts, it's a sore subject, a time when I felt stuck, as if I had no choice, as if I couldn't breathe.

The Latin root of inspiration is *inspirare*, meaning to blow into, to breathe upon. The root of *spirare* is spirit. The English uses of inspire give it the meaning "to influence, move, or guide through divine or supernatural agency or power." One needs to have a clear passage for the spirit to enter, to move and guide us, as opposed to a blocked passageway, like I had at the Latin cuisine restaurant, or when I dated the woman who kept buying me presents. Thank goodness she lived a plane-ride away; during that period, any divine spirits were blocked, obstructed by a mass of worry, of guilt, of resentment, towards the gift-giver, towards myself for accepting her presents.

After messaging on OkCupid, the gift-giver and I had talked on the phone. During the first minute of our conversation, my gut said no. Her nasal voice and thick Long Island accent reminded me of the fast-talking mean girls who pushed me around in grade school. And the gift-giver, in her online profile photo, looked like the leader of the mean girl pack, both tall and thin with long brown hair in a ponytail. In fifth grade, the pack leader asked if she could cut in front of me while I waited in line for the school bus. I said no. "You're so snotty," she said. "Maybe that's why you have no friends."

At least I had boundaries.

Although the gift-giver made me laugh, asked questions, listened to my answers and asked follow-up questions, I told her I didn't want more than a friendship, the distance was too much, but we could be special friends. She said she'd love to be special friends. She asked where I wanted to travel. "Antarctica," I said. She said, "I'll take you there," and I said, "You'd take a friend?" and she said, "I take my friends lots of places." We talked daily. I liked talking to her. She always answered the phone. She told me her father dropped dead of a heart attack when she was fourteen, right in front of her. She could barely speak about it, and I told her about my mother, killed in a car accident, over two decades before, when I was twenty-five. The gift-giver read my stories, begged me to send more.

Maybe I gave the gift-giver too much credit for picking up the phone.

The gift-giver made arrangements to stay at a fancy hotel in Asheville, the hotel where Obama stayed. Two days before her visit, she sent flowers and asked if I was still only interested in a friendship. I tried to convince myself that even though she reminded me of the mean girls who taunted me, even though her nasal voice got on my nerves, I needed to stop judging her based on past prejudices. So what if I wasn't even attracted to her photos? Perhaps I needed to try something different. "If it feels unusual," my psychologist friend said, "don't run. It might mean you're breaking out of your old patterns."

At the airport, the gift-giver hugged me for a minute too long and said, "It's about time!" She touched my hand while I drove. I slowly pulled it away. Later that day, after walking my dog, the gift-giver wanted to take me to dinner, wherever I wanted to go. "Invite your friends," she said. Two friends accompanied us to a fancy tapas restaurant and the bill came to $300. The gift-giver slapped her credit card on the table. My friends insisted on paying their share—they had their own money, but the gift-giver said, "It's on me."

The gift-giver said she could go back to the hotel, the hotel she'd already paid for, but if I wanted to keep hanging out, she'd be fine with that. I was a little drunk from two martinis and invited her back to my house and one thing led to the next and she held me and stayed over, and the next morning she told me how happy she was, how she was my family, how I'd never have to feel alone again, how we were soulmates. She insisted on taking me on a shopping spree, "anywhere you want to go."

"You don't have to buy me anything, " I said. "I have my own money. Remember? I'm a college professor."

"But I want to," she said.

"It makes me feel uncomfortable," I said. "Like there are strings attached." Despite my protests, we went to REI. "I need to get boots," I said.

"Get what you want," she said. "I insist!"

"I don't need your money," I said. I didn't find boots that fit, but I tried on an expensive fleece jacket and a hat, and the gift-giver grabbed them and threw her credit card down at the register.

The gift-giver said I should enjoy life. She wanted to have fun and watch movies and go on walks with my dog. She said she couldn't wait to take me around the world. She asked if it was okay to stay another three days. I hesitated. She said, "Do you want me to stay or not?"

I told her yes but felt overwhelmed. "Maybe we should take a break," I said.

She went to the gym at the fancy hotel. "Might as well," she said, "get something for all the money I paid."

A month after meeting in person, the gift-giver asked me to move to Chicago, where she ran her family's foundation. She said she'd support me, so I could spend my time writing. I held my heart, now beating out of control, overcome with angst. She said I shouldn't be afraid. I told her I liked teaching; I worked hard to get where I was in my career. "Besides," I said, "you don't even know me."

"I'm sure," she said, "you're the one. I just know."

Maybe I fit into the box she created for what she wanted in a partner, a confined box with a limited amount of breathing room, a coffin of sorts.

I told a friend about the gift-giver, how I didn't know how to *not* accept her presents, just like I didn't know how *not* to accept her attention. She said, "Give her my number! Giving gifts is one of the five love languages." Based on the book by Gary Chapman, he writes, "Don't mistake this love language for materialism. The receiver of gifts thrives on the love, thoughtfulness, and effort behind the gift…the perfect gift or gesture shows that you are known, are cared for, and you are prized above whatever was sacrificed to bring the gift to you." Yet the iPad and fleece jacket didn't necessarily make me feel cared for or prized. They made me feel like a prostitute.

The gift-giver owned a giant house near Lake Michigan. She told me she felt a dark energy in her living room. I felt it too. I feared that room, the heaviness, especially at night. Before I arrived, two different paintings on her walls had crashed down in her house, on separate nights, at 3 a.m.

At the gift-giver's house, I couldn't sleep, which wasn't a big surprise. Now I took Ativan to sleep and forgot about my breath, barely inhaling and exhaling through the tiny passageways to my lungs, to my heart.

Three months after we met, the gift-giver took me to a five-star resort in Puerto Rico. At breakfast the first morning, she said she had made reservations at a five-star hotel in San Francisco for my spring break. I told her I didn't need to stay at a fancy hotel. I asked if we could pick a hotel together. "I'd be happy to pay half," I said. "I'm fine with the Holiday Inn."

"Forget it. Just forget it," she said. "You're so selfish and ungrateful! I'll invite another friend." She wouldn't look at me, got up and paid the bill. She said she needed to take a break.

"Please don't go," I said. "I'm sorry."

She went shopping and left me in the hotel room, which now felt like a prison. I cried and gasped and wanted to die. I texted the gift-giver: *Please come back*. I apologized again. I didn't even know who I was.

An hour later, she came back with a bar of chocolate and a card: *Thanks for coming to Puerto Rico with me!*

She mentioned an Alaska rowing trip she wanted to take me on. "I'm not a great rower," I said. She said, "You'll have plenty of time to get in shape before then."

Maybe I was selfish and ungrateful like she had said. Besides, I'd never stayed at a luxury resort; the bulk of my paid lodging had been at cheap motels off the interstate. As a kid, my family took long car rides to tourist destinations like Old Sturbridge Village, where costumed actors reenacted 19th-century life, and Lancaster, Pennsylvania, where we stopped off at an Amish salami factory. Despite our exhaustion from the car rides, my mother refused to spend money on a motel, so we slept in our turquoise station wagon at the side of the road. At thirteen, my parents took me on a package tour of Europe. It was free to take a kid along. The night we arrived in Amsterdam, instead of getting a hotel, my mother, father and I sat in a freezing rail station all night and I had to pee, but the bathroom was locked until morning and by the time the attendant opened the door, I almost knocked her down.

Now at the hotel, the gift-giver and I both took Ativan before going to sleep. Even with the Ativan, she stayed up all night playing

Candy Crush and shopping online. I didn't sleep well either, and in the morning, when the gift-giver asked if I wanted time to write, I said no. I wasn't inspired to do anything but drink coffee and go back to sleep.

Every so often a student in my creative writing class arrives without their homework. "I wasn't inspired," they'd say. I'd ask if they'd come into a math class or an art history class and say the same thing. At times you have to clear the way for the spirit to move you, to invite the spirit in, to pat the seat next to you and say, *come sit beside me*. A well-known phrase in the writing world is: *Writing is 90% perspiration and 10% inspiration*. The Latin root of *perspire* means to blow or breathe constantly. As if feeding a fire, we could blow constantly and call the spirit in, and keep blowing until the fire ignites. And if my fire won't light, I force myself to free-write without stopping. Eventually a kernel of an idea shows up and corridors open, making way for the spirit to enter and take over.

Five years after breaking up with the gift-giver, I took a workshop titled, "Connect with the Spirit World," instructed by a famous psychic medium. The first day I sat across from a classmate, and we exchanged personal items. The instructor asked us to feel the energy from the item and tell our partner something about them. I held my partner's engagement ring. She held my watch. I closed my eyes and a cheese wedge appeared. And wouldn't go away. "All I see is a cheese wedge," I said. She said, "I *love* cheese. All kinds of cheese. I even took a wedge of cheese with me from home and had a piece before breakfast." She went on about her favorite cheeses. She closed her eyes and squeezed my watch. "You're very organized," she said, which is true. Because of my mother's hoarding, clutter makes me nervous and organization makes me feel in control. I love to make lists: To-do lists, gratitude lists, friend lists.

To loosen us up, the instructor blared 90's dance music, and I skipped and jumped. Two minutes into the song, I felt a sharp pain in my calf, as if a bullet ripped through it. I hobbled back to my seat, not sure what happened to my leg.

I asked a curly-haired woman if she'd partner with me for another exercise. We sat across from each other. One of us had to be the receiver, the other the psychic medium. "Tell your partner the name of a dead person," the instructor said, "and the relationship you had with him or her." I gave my partner information about my mother, and she closed her eyes and began to cry. "Your mother is so sorry," she said. "She wishes she was more affectionate with you. This is why you're having a hard time finding a stable relationship." I nodded, cried, tried not to worry about my leg. "Your mother wants you to jump," she said. "Do everything you want. Don't hold back."

"I did just jump," I said, massaging my leg. "I think I tore a calf muscle!"

I asked my partner if she had experience doing this kind of thing. She gave me her shiny card: *Violetta, Psychic Medium*.

For the remainder of the workshop, I couldn't walk. Along with a big woman with a broken toe, I waited for a golf-cart to shuttle me around. Before I jumped, my calf muscle felt like a rubberband that could snap at any moment. But I let myself get carried away by the dance music and ignored my injury, just like I ignored my gut when it came to the gift-giver. *She's not for you!* my gut screamed. I tried to override it with reasoning, contrary to what the famous psychic medium told us: "Thoughts only get in the way of your gut and intuition. Let the spirit in without judgment and thought."

Perhaps, because of my mother's lack of affection, I didn't feel worthy of receiving it. Instead, I invited partners into my life like the woman who kept buying me presents. Maybe the gift-giver, I had thought, could fill the void left by my mother, who threw crumbs of affection, mostly when I drove her to shopping malls. My mother didn't seem interested in what I did, even when, as a teenager, I rode my banana-seat bicycle on a busy five-lane highway.

The gift-giver's present to my dog—a real cow bone, caused my dog's tooth to crack, which she had to get pulled. The vet told me dogs shouldn't be biting on anything harder than their teeth, and a cow bone is harder. The night of her surgery, my dog was zonked, but the next day she ate well and ran around like her usual self. On the phone, the gift-giver insisted I stay with my dog and not go out to dinner with a friend. "But my dog is fine," I said. She said, "This is indicative of how you'd treat a partner. You'd just leave them alone after a major surgery."

At the Latin cuisine restaurant, I thought I viewed the last scene of life, before the curtains closed, and even though my date helped to save my life, I only wanted a friendship, similar to what I said at first to the woman who kept buying me presents. Towards the end of our relationship, the gift-giver mentioned she wanted to take me on a lesbian cruise for my birthday. I told her I wasn't sure about the cruise. I told her I get seasick. What I wouldn't tell her: I didn't want to be stuck with her in a tiny cabin while she played Candy Crush. I didn't give a damn if Billie Jean King was scheduled to appear on the cruise.

By the time the cruise embarked, I had broken up with the gift-giver. My body was a tangled mass of nerves. When I drove away for the last time, nine months after meeting her, not only did the road open up, but so did my breath. A month later, she sent my father, who she had spent a total of two hours with, an expensive fruit basket on Thanksgiving. My father said, "She's aggressive, isn't she?"

In the "Connect with the Spirit World" workshop, the instructor said we needed to forgive others before we could forgive ourselves—the only way to fully open our hearts. I had already forgiven my mother. But now I had to forgive the woman who kept buying me gifts. This was her love language, perhaps the only language she knew.

After I almost died in the Latin cuisine restaurant, I walked out into the sun and sat on a bench with my date. I hugged her, thanked her for saving my life, for taking charge. She said, "Next time you're on a date, maybe you should only order soup."

On a street corner nearby, a young boy strummed his guitar while singing a Johnny Cash song. I began to cry but wasn't sure why. Maybe I was grateful for the music pulsing through my body, or for the opportunity to jump, wholeheartedly, back into my life. Or maybe I was grateful for the gift of breath—unhindered, free from the weight of fancy dinners, Apple products and five star hotels.

THE ISLAND *of* TSK

IN HER LATE FIFTIES, MY GREAT-GRANDMOTHER, allergic to Novocain, died in a dentist's chair. Her daughter, my grandma Becky, suffered from a lifelong depression and spent the last year of her life in a hospital bed, unable to walk or eat. My mother, her only child, died in the passenger seat of a Nissan Sentra. This is my bad luck lineage.

Grandma Becky never learned to swim, but she sat for hours at Brighton Beach and watched the waves crash against the shore, the tankers out at sea. Even after I learned to swim, Grandma Becky warned me to stay close to the shoreline. "The waves," she said. "So dangerous. They pull you out and make you disappear."

I can't recall my grandmother ever laughing, only tsking with disappointment. When she brushed sand off our chopped liver sandwiches at the beach. When she argued with my mother. When I interviewed her, two years before she died, I learned about her loveless marriage with my grandpa Harry. Harry Blank. "I made do," she said. At twenty, she gave birth to my mother. At twenty-one, she found herself pregnant again. "I wasn't ready for another child. Not yet," she said. "We didn't have the money." My grandfather supported whatever decision she made. She later learned that the abortion left her infertile. At least the abortionist didn't kill her. But he might have killed her spirit. "Of course I wanted more children," she said, followed by a string of tsks. "Such a shame."

"Do you think," I said, "your life would have been different if you had another child?"

"I wanted three children. How many my mother had," she said, looking off in the distance. "One's not enough."

My mother had suspected Grandma Becky engaged in an ongoing affair with my grandfather's best friend. She told this to my sister. At the age of twelve, my mother ran into the couple after Grandma Becky said she had to run an errand. My mother didn't have siblings to talk to and didn't want to reveal this information to friends or relatives, so she carried the weight of this secret alone.

Perhaps, through art, my mother made sense of her life; she studied painting in college with abstract expressionists Mark Rothko and Robert Motherwell. I imagine her standing in front of a blank canvas, excited to create a different world to inhabit, a world where she could escape the pressures of growing up female in the 1940's and 50's. In a photo from her college days, she laughs with four friends in the Hunter College cafeteria, conveying a freedom I never saw when she was my mother.

On Sundays my father drove our family to Brighton Beach in a turquoise station wagon to visit my grandparents. Along the way, we held our noses when passing Starrett City, a new development off the Belt Parkway, built atop a Brooklyn garbage dump. Grandpa Harry and Grandma Becky lived in a Neptune Avenue apartment complex occupied mostly by Russian immigrants who sat on long orange benches. The smell of buckwheat groats permeated their apartment. My grandfather kneeled by his liquor cabinet and poured himself vodka shots. "Good," he said, swigging down the alcohol. "Vodka good." He sat on the plastic-covered couch in the living room, his arms crossed, watching *Bonanza*, *Gunsmoke* and *Little House on the Prairie* on their console television.

My mother bickered in Yiddish with my grandmother, and every so often, Grandma Becky yelled my mother's name. Despite the tension, I loved being there. I especially loved learning magic tricks, using a deck of cards, from my grandfather.

Sometimes I stayed over by myself. Grandma Becky and I walked to the beach and set up chairs and an umbrella while metal detector men scanned the sand for coins. I loved the expansiveness of space, the horizon, the clouds. We strolled on the boardwalk to Coney Island, where I played skee ball and climbed atop a mechanical horse. It jiggled and shook and I held on tight and laughed—the closest I had come to galloping on a real horse.

Similar to many women of her day, my grandmother never learned to drive. Trapped in a loveless marriage, stuck in her depression. My mother never learned to drive either. In Brooklyn, subways ran all the time, but in the suburbs, my father served as my mother's chauffeur.

My mother's creative spark might have been hijacked by her era and situation, but I didn't let her hijack mine, although when I told her of my plans to attend graduate school for art, she screamed: "You don't go to graduate school for art! You go for medicine or law!" It took another eight years to find the confidence to apply to graduate school for writing; in the meantime, I filmed Grandma Becky in her Brighton Beach apartment. The last time I traveled to see her there, the only other person on the subway jerked off beneath a newspaper. I switched cars. I asked my grandmother to smile for the camera. She said, "Why do you want to film me?" She forced a smile and waved. She said she had enough of this life. I asked her to pose while she looked through a magnifying glass. Her eye enlarged, the same eye that took in the expansive Soviet landscape, the eye that now felt better closed.

Before she checked into the hospital for the last time, Grandma Becky lived with a Polish aide. One immigrant wheeling around another. Already Parkinson's Disease plagued my grandmother. Already diabetes plagued her. Already stomach ulcers plagued her.

Already my mother was dead. Already my grandmother couldn't get out of bed without help. The aide complained about being woken in the middle of the night, so my grandmother limited her liquid intake. One morning she passed out and had to be rushed to the hospital for dehydration. She never went back home. She moved from nursing home bed to a hospital bed. Back and forth. Musical beds. A situation worthy of many tsks.

The hospital called at four in the morning: *Becky Blank expired.* Like the due date of a library book? Or a magazine subscription?

What I still have of my grandmother's: a little hammer she used to break pills, the wooden bowl and chopper she used to cut up string beans and fried onions and eggs to make her string bean salad, and a set of fine china and crystal glasses. What I still have are memories of my grandmother stuck in her Brighton Beach apartment, a defeated life.

What I still have of my mother's: a sketchpad of drawings from her college days, and super-8 films that my father took in their first year of marriage. My mother, red-haired and freckled, smiles and waves to the camera, excited for her new life, finally able to fill in her Blank. But this new life overwhelmed her. She didn't tsk, but she hummed—a hum to comfort herself, a hum to ease the sorrow of abandoning her art, and perhaps, herself.

I've also felt stuck—in relationships, in jobs, in anxiety; yet because of the greater freedoms of my generation, I've had options: an option not to marry or bear children, to love who I want, to go to therapy, where I've learned to understand and manage my anxiety and bad luck lineage. During the thirteen years I had lived in Manhattan, when anxiety overtook me, I boarded the Staten Island Ferry. Lower Manhattan drifted out of sight and the seagulls squawked and the wind whipped through my hair, and I pretended to be a tourist; on occasion, when passing by Ellis Island, I imagined myself an immigrant about to discover new sights and smells. By the time I stepped off the ferry, I was ready to get back to my life.

Even though the Island of Tsk is never completely out of sight, it doesn't stare me down, like it did Grandma Becky. Towards the end of her life, she repeated, "I'm done already. I don't want this life no more." When her best friend Bilmes, known only by her last name, died of lung cancer (a cigarette always dangled from her lips), Grandma Becky locked her ivory mah jongg pieces in a mothball closet. On Ocean Avenue I saw her walk for the last time, each step a victory, pushing a squeaky metal cart. A month before she died, in a stuffy hospital room overlooking a glass-strewn lot, I clipped her nails. She asked if I was married.

"Nah," I said. "I'm in no rush."

I rubbed Vaseline on her lips, gave her an ice cube to suck on.

"I looked out the window," she said, "and saw you riding on a white horse."

I held her hand, her grip strong as it was when Yiddish chatter skimmed the surf at Brighton Beach, when she held my tiny torso up while I screamed and splashed and pretended to swim.

COOL *as* PATTY HEARST

TWELVE YEARS OLD, captive in my bedroom with frilly curtains and a flowery bedspread, the image of Patty Hearst flashed across the TV screen, a grainy videotape photo of her in a beret, a machine gun cradled in her arms. *One day*, I thought, *I want to be as cool as Patty Hearst looks in that photo.* Let's hear it for the debutante turned revolutionary.

Before I knew I liked girls, strong girls, the bank image of Patty Hearst sent tingles through my body. Twelve years later, while traveling in Northern Ireland, I came upon a similar image, a painted mural on the side of a bombed out building in Belfast. A woman in camouflage wearing a beret, a machine-gun in her hands. There's something about a woman with a beret and a machine gun—a woman who knows how to get what she wants. Not that I'm an advocate of violence, but as the mural proclaimed: *You Can Kill the Revolutionary but Not the Revolution.* Later that day at a pub, a seventeen-year old kid, thrilled to speak to an American, a rarity at the time, asked me what I was doing in Belfast. "You must be mad," he said. Because I had been stuck in my frilly pink bedroom for so long, I longed to live on the edge. He told me about his brother hauled off to prison for bombing a department store. "When he gets out," he said, "he'll do it again." He asked which side I was on, if I supported the British Army. I wasn't on either side, mostly because I didn't know the full story but told him about my job at an Irish-American newspaper in New York, where the editors supported the IRA and loved Ronald Reagan. "Reagan is a good man," the kid said. I didn't tell him that the more Reagan talked about the Communists who were out to get us, the less I believed him. At the newspaper, if we had extra space before going to press, the editor, an older leprechaun-looking Irishman who giggled, pulled a letter from a stockpile of fake letters comparing abortion doctors with Nazi war criminals.

And this was the 80's and people said hitching in Ireland was safe, even for a woman traveling alone, and I thought, *Great! I'll save some money and meet the locals!* I wore a pea-coat, beret, green khakis and a big backpack, and stuck my thumb out. A woman with a small child stopped and drove me twenty miles up the road. Then I got another ride with two middle-aged women who said, "Top of the morning to you" and "You're American! That's brilliant!" I was on a roll and stuck out my thumb for a third time. An older man with a big balding head and rotted teeth pulled over, and I ducked my body into his tiny car. I couldn't understand much with his thick accent and gravelly voice but nodded when he spoke. A hairy mole grew from his neck. He asked if I hitched a lot. When he pulled over to let me out in front of a youth hostel, he kissed me on the lips. Stunned and baffled, I wiped my lips and took the train from there on out.

At the hostel I met a woman who served in the U.S. Army, stationed in Germany and on break. She loved Ronald Reagan and believed the dollar was strong because of his leadership. That night she told me about a friend at the army base who had given her a massage. Later she learned the friend was a lesbian. When she found out she felt disgusted. "Imagine that," she said. "A lesbian massaging me. Gross." Can one be grossed out by physical touch, only in hindsight? I didn't say a word, because I was in love with the Englishwoman, who also wore army boots and a beret. We were having a secret affair, so secret that we never talked about what was going on, only about the men in our lives.

Patty Hearst served two years in prison for driving the bank-heist getaway car, released early because she claimed her captors brainwashed her. Maybe they did. I think about the connections between brainwashing and desire—if we truly want something, or want something we've been brainwashed to want. I knew it was bad to like girls because people said terrible things about fags and dykes and queers. I hadn't even known of any, not until college. When I told my mother I met a friend from my hometown, a gay man, she said, "Oh, he's probably just pretending to be gay."

Fifteen years after she married, a friend called to say she was getting divorced. She said, "You're the only one who told me not to get married, and you were right." When she had told me about her impending marriage, I asked if there was passion between her and her fiancé. "Not really," she had said. "But that's not the most important thing." "Don't do it!" I replied. She said that during the first part of the marriage, despite the lack of passion, she felt so normal, so settled. She was somebody's wife. At the same time, all I wanted was to meet a guy, get married and settle down; instead I dated women but hoped I wasn't really a lesbian.

Patty Hearst, kidnapped at nineteen, was a rebellious teenager who told a nun at Catholic school to go to hell. At nineteen, I traveled alone through Israel, Greece and Turkey. I didn't shave my legs in Europe; I always hated that I *had* to shave them. At fifteen, I argued with my mother when she insisted I shave my legs for my cousin's wedding. We compromised when I agreed to wear black tights. In Europe, none of the Europeans shaved, so why would I? Back at college, I shaved stripes into my hairy legs—vertical stripes in one leg, horizontal in the other.

Perhaps army boots and berets are overrated. Now that I'm a college professor, I prefer to blend in, to not call attention to myself. I try to make a difference by teaching students to question authority, to consider our truths and where they come from, to speak up in the face of injustice. And when minds open, when ideas take shape, the light is brighter, and louder, than any grenade thrown on enemy soil.

THOSE FRIDAY AFTERNOONS

ONE OF THE HEAVILY ROTATED 45 singles my sixth-grade teacher, Mr. Diamond, played on Friday afternoons was Helen Reddy's "I am Woman." He introduced the song the day he taught us about Women's Liberation, Gloria Steinem, and Shirley Chisholm—who ran for president the year before. After school, I ran home, my Pippi Longstocking braids flapping from side to side, to tell my family I was a "Women's Libber." I didn't care that my brother mimicked my declaration, hand on his hip and all. I didn't understand how all women wouldn't advocate for equal rights.

On Friday afternoons, Mr. Diamond let us do what we wanted. Half the class played spin-the-bottle, the other half sat at our desks—reading, talking, working on projects; we were the outsiders who moved our desks out of the way so the insiders could spin the Coke bottle on gray-speckled linoleum tiles. I can't remember what Mr. Diamond did during those afternoons other than change records; he could have been grading papers, or writing lesson plans. A short stocky guy with a ponytail, he tried to come off as our cool teacher, but the spin-the-bottle kids made fun of his dandruff, though I never noticed it.

While I molded cats and dogs out of red clay for shoebox dioramas, from the corner of my eye, I saw Patty Ward and Mitchell Feinberg on their knees in an awkward embrace, lips chafing together. After the kiss, Patty slowly wiped spit away with her sleeve, as if wiping off a piece of magic.

Patty, who once tried to trip me in the hallway, and Mitchell, who asked me during a quiet lull on the morning bus to school, "Where's your tits?" I focused on the finely cut lawn out the window. In gym class, I wore a striped training bra and tried to hide my body in a locker before changing into a one-piece gym-suit.

Content to roll and pinch clay to create ears and tails, I had no desire to be part of the circle (not that I'd ever be invited). Why would I want to kiss Mitchell Feinberg or Stephen Calhoon, who slobbered over Melanie Gross?

Marked as an introverted loner by second grade, I gave up on making friends at school. Why bother when I'd have to endure wrath from the same kids until high school graduation? I found solace in art and music—I played guitar and wrote songs about my poodles, spent hours in a makeshift darkroom, and made animated super 8 films of clay figures. To get away from the constant commotion in my house—blaring televisions, screaming, fights with my siblings—I hid in my bedroom closet next to a pile of photography magazines. I knew my situation would have to change once my context changed, once I could be myself amongst a new peer group. It already had. During summers, until I was almost twelve, I attended a local recreation program. I'd bond with my summer friend, Wendy Godfrey, and together we were the confident captains of the kickball team, the popular duo who sat together while we wove lanyard necklaces.

Because we attended different junior high schools, three years had passed before Wendy and I crossed paths again; she sat two seats in front of me in my high school social studies class. I didn't know how to navigate the situation, so I pretended not to recognize her and passed by her desk, until she grabbed my arm. "Don't you remember me?" she asked.

I feigned surprise. "Oh, Wendy!"

She said she wanted to hang out. I said okay, but soon she discovered I'd been marked. In the cafeteria, she sat with a group of girls who had known me since elementary school. I sat nearby, alone, eating burnt lasagna. One of the girls pointed at me and called me a "queer-o faggot." Wendy laughed along with the group.

At sixteen, I graduated a year early from high school and moved into a college dorm, one of the happiest days of my life. Now I was an upbeat artsy chick. Boys invited me on walks and flirted. A month into the school year, a hippie boy asked me to be his girlfriend. I told him I felt flattered but thought of our connection as a friendship, which wasn't entirely true. I wasn't ready to date him because another boy had pursued me and he was cuter and more confident. Unlike in sixth-grade when no boys liked me, now I had options. I made sure to tell the cute boy about how I rejected the hippie, and he said oh, I could have sworn you two would get together, and that night we kissed.

My new boyfriend made fun of my suitemate—a self-proclaimed bisexual feminist. When he waved goodbye to her, he said, "*Byyyyeee*," then turned to me and whispered, "I mean *bi*-sexual," and we laughed and kissed. Six years later I'd claim the same label for myself, but for now, my early feminist education was buried underneath heavy layers of mainstream culture. Between six-grade and freshman year of college, I learned, directly or indirectly, from teachers, peers, family, television, that feminists were angry women who couldn't get a man, gay people were pariahs, and attention from any male, especially a boyfriend, affirmed womanhood. I disregarded Helen Reddy's proclamation about being strong and invincible. Now my strength came from male adoration. After a month of kissing and running away from my new boyfriend—he wanted more than I wanted to give—he moved onto a blonde skinny dancer. I moved onto alcohol.

One night I attended a hall party, and after downing my third cup of grain-alcohol punch, I kept telling anyone who'd listen: "Wow! This drink is *so* good. I don't think there's any alcohol in it!"

A Deadhead boy invited me to get stoned with him and said something about the "radical feminists," and I thought about the spiky-haired girls in motorcycle jackets who hopped around to Devo and Talking Heads on dance night in the student union, always a serious expression on their faces.

When Jerry Garcia finished singing "Friend of the Devil," I ran back to the punch bowl.

I vaguely remember getting sick. A friend dressed me in her white nightgown, and another friend hoisted me over his shoulder and walked me back to my room and put me to bed. The next morning at breakfast I bumped into my hall-mate. He stopped in his tracks and said, "What are you doing here? I thought you were dead!" He saw me carried away in a white gown, but there was more alcohol, so he kept drinking. We both laughed. This was my idea of liberation, even if it meant almost dying. All through college, I went to parties and kissed boys, and they followed me around, and I mostly ran away at the end of the night. As long as I was an object of desire, I felt a sense of worth—in retrospect, a bankrupt, disembodied sense of worth.

It took a few more decades to understand that empowerment doesn't need to come from the adoration of men, or women. In grad school, I served as a teaching assistant for a women's studies course. On the first day, the professor asked students if they considered themselves feminists. Along with most of the class, I didn't raise my hand. Instead I slunk down in my desk, not wanting to be associated with the word's connotations: radical, man-hating, screaming in the streets while holding up signs. The professor explained that the basic tenet of the word *feminism* is that all genders should have equal rights and opportunities. She told us how mainstream culture has taught us it's a scary word because strong women are perceived as a threat to many men, and women. Ever since, I've slowly unearthed the buried-over inspiration I found in sixth-grade, the day Mr. Diamond held up a copy of *Ms.* and told us that a woman's identity didn't have to be dependent on her marital status. I sat at my desk, chin in hand, mesmerized.

As one of the organizers for the 2017 Women's March on Asheville, I devised a playlist for the event, placing "I am Woman" at the top. When Helen Reddy's words echoed from the speakers—"I am Strong, I am Invincible"—many of the ten-thousand strong crowd sang along and raised their fists, reminding me of the day I ran home, excited to share my newfound "women's libber" status, when I didn't care about being part of the spin-the-bottle circle, when I had no desire to kiss random boys, when I was perfectly happy to mold red clay into whatever the hell I pleased, when I had the power to mold myself into whomever the hell I pleased.

THE MICROWAVE

Now that we have a microwave, my mother has no need for a conventional oven. She uses the microwave to boil water for spaghetti, cook chicken and steak dinners, and defrost frozen milk. Every day she takes home two or three little parcels of milk from her kindergarten class, the leftovers from absent students.

When my mother pushes the *on* button, the purr of the microwave resonates throughout the house. "We're all going to get cancer!" I scream. "I feel the radiation." I run from the kitchen into my bedroom, where I watch television, nonstop.

I tell my mother it takes less time to boil water using our stovetop oven, but she likes the convenience of the microwave. Sometimes she browns cheap chuck steak in the regular oven, and me and my siblings fight over what part we'll get. "I want the bone!" I scream. My father mixes cottage cheese with ketchup and says he loves the combination. He takes an ice cube from the freezer and sucks on it. "Very good cube," he says. "Tastes like meat."

When I realize my tongue sandwiches are made from actual cow's tongue, I never eat tongue again. And when chicken bones remind me of the pet chickens I once had, I go through a no-chicken eating phase.

My brother's room is across from mine, and for the past week, he's locked himself in it. Because he complained of chest pains, my father dragged him to our obese Austrian doctor. But the doctor called my brother a hypochondriac. My father bangs on my brother's door and says, "Get out of your room and stop pulling on yourself! Run around the block a few times!" Two days later, my brother comes out of his room and gasps for breath. He is rushed to the hospital with a collapsed lung.

In the school cafeteria, I pull an oily sardine sandwich wrapped in tin foil from a brown paper bag, four pennies for milk at the bag's bottom, mixed in with crumbled cookies. I love sardines, even though kids sneer, point and ask, "What's that?" I answer, "Tuna fish."

My father is summoned by my mother's shrieks. She tried to cook a hard-boiled egg in the microwave but pressure yanked the oven door open. Yolk-splatter covers every visible kitchen surface.

GIRL *in the* MAROON VELVET GOWN

MAYBE I SWING MY ARMS AND HIPS AND LEGS a little too much, maybe I smile too big and jump too high, but Mathew Goldberg, who asked me to dance at my brother's Bar Mitzvah, stands still, arms snapped to his sides. "Forget it," he says.

Despite the "Rock Around the Clock" guitar solo and the couples swinging all around, my world falls silent. I skulk back to the dais, but not before tripping on my maroon velvet gown and stumbling into my chair.

Somewhere on Long Island's South Shore, there's a Sweet Sixteen dance contest. Couples are eliminated until two couples remain. It's me and Hugh Wunderman, Leslie Wunderman's brother. Leslie Wunderman, better known as 80's pop icon Taylor Dane, whose hits include "Tell it to my Heart." *To hell with you, Mathew Goldberg.* Now the DJ plays Abba's "Dancing Queen" and Hugh grabs my hands and swings me around and I swing him around and we're sweating and laughing and clapping and following each other's moves and the song ends and the judge declares us the winning couple.

I am the dancing queen. Thank you Abba. Two years later I'm at Radio City Music Hall and Abba performs in one-piece white suits, silver studding around the edges, moving in unison, big Swedish smiles on their faces. *Knowing me, knowing you it's the best I can do.* Ah ha.

Forget it, Mathew Goldberg says.

The Peppermint Lounge, New York City. I'm with a handsome Brit, and we're standing on the edge of the dance floor. Madonna sings about how she's gonna dress you up in her love and a long-blonde haired woman wearing a purple tank top sprints onto the empty floor and sways her arms and smiles and twirls and kicks up her legs and the Brit sneers at the woman and says, "What a nut." I agree. What a nut. We both laugh. *Do you really want to hurt me?* Boy George asks. *Do you really want to make me cry?*

She leapt through the air as if her life depended on it; we stood, our arms folded into our chests, as if already dead.

Years later, Mathew Goldberg sends me a Facebook friend request. I accept. He's an architect. And gay. He's been with his partner for over a decade. Maybe leaving me on the dance floor was the best thing he could have done. A lesson. Just because someone invites you to dance doesn't mean they'll stay with you. Perhaps it's enough to be led there, to join in with others, or perhaps go solo, to say, *The hell with you* (and thank you), *Mathew Goldberg*.

A THREESOME *with* TIME

Although I liked the attention, I hadn't considered Abigail as girlfriend material—the age of a legal adult stood between us. At least that's how I saw her thirty-three years to my fifty-two. "If you were closer to my age," she said, "I'd totally go for you." Our feet shuffled through fallen leaves, reds and oranges shimmering above, and I took a breath of crisp October air.

A week before at a lesbian get-together, a group of women had gathered around Abigail, the new girl in town. She waved her long fingers and brushed hair from her face and spoke about the politics and syntax of French surrealist poetry—the focus of her dissertation.

"You remind me of me, a mini-me," I said, both of us New Yorkers from the same Jewish stock, writers and professors. Abigail responded, "I'm honored to be the mini-you." My anxiety level shot up, the pleasant kind that leads to giddiness. I saw our interaction as a healthy flirtation, if not a little bit of an ego boost. At first glance, Abigail could pass for a teenage girl in skinny jeans. I even referred to her as "The Little Girl." Maybe I used this phrase so I wouldn't take her seriously, the same way my father referred to a woman he had begun to date as "The Lady," three months after my mother died.

Abigail decided to take a break from New York and check out the North Carolina mountains. A serious poet, she had written an award-winning book with blurbs on the back by three famous poets. I asked how she got such a glowing testimonial from one of the poets, a Pulitzer-Prize winner. Abigail said she learned where the poet lived, showed up on her doorstep and asked if she'd look at her poems.

I'm not sure Abigail was the mini-me; she was the most ambitious person I had ever met.

While Abigail and I walked in the woods and talked about poetry and French theorists, her stare slid the peephole of my heart open, but I looked away and said I had to get home and grade papers.

Amid reading student stories about dying grandparents, I couldn't stop thinking about Abigail. I texted and asked if she wanted to go to a pumpkin carving party. Thirty minutes later, she held a bottle of wine and hugged me, the bottle knocking at my spine. I pointed at a Japanese Maple tree in my yard, some leaves green, others orange and red against the blue sky. "Soon the tree will be on fire," I said.

We drank the wine, an Italian cabernet mentioned in a poem she loved. She had a copy of the poem and read it to me—maybe she had multiple copies of the poem and this is how she courted women. She started to pour more wine and asked, "Do we have to go to the party?"

"I already told friends I'd go to the party," I said, and picked up my pumpkin. At the party, I stood close to Abigail, our backs leaning against outdoor deck railing, her fork swooping the last of my potato salad. We posed for a photo, our arms around each other, and after the camera snapped, we didn't let go for a minute or two. We chatted with others but kept hovering back, and by the time I pulled into my driveway, by the time the engine quieted, Abigail hadn't moved from the passenger seat. "I don't want to leave," she said. "I'm having such a good time with you."

I opened my door. "I have to get to sleep," I said. Abigail got out of the car and we hugged. She drove off.

At dinner the next evening, she told me about living on a small French island and staying alone in a haunted house. She couldn't sleep but wrote poetry all night. She said she liked to put herself in uncomfortable situations. That made two of us, because the situation right then terrified me. She rubbed her leg against mine, touched my arm and said, "Would you sleep with me once?"

I spotted vague creases by her eyes, which made me feel a little better out in public with her. "Why once?"

"Because I figure," she said, "that's all I could get from you."

Did she use those words on other women? Two colleagues walked in the restaurant.

I didn't invite Abigail inside my house, but she followed me to my back door. "I was hoping," she said, "I'd at least get a goodnight kiss."

On my porch, I took Abigail's hand and we sat on the concrete step, the Japanese Maple standing over us, hundreds of small delicate leaves with pointy lobes that spread outward like fingers on a palm. Hundreds of fingers creeping towards me, perhaps fingers that only wanted to caress me, and heaven knows I needed caressing.

Abigail moved closer and held my hand in hers. "It's getting cold," she said. "Don't you have a couch or something?"

I cracked up at her brashness. "Yes, I have a couch or something." Unbeknownst to me, Abigail had left her computer in my kitchen before we left for the restaurant; she'd have a reason to come into my house, if the couch line didn't work.

I tried to remain vertical but it didn't take much to get me horizontal, with her on top. Right after we kissed, she said, "Do you want children?"

I lifted my head. "We don't even know each other!"

She talked about her ticking clock and wanting to find a partner. She asked again if I had ever wanted kids. I told her there were times I did want children but it was more important to find a healthy relationship. We kissed and groped for the next two hours and now I didn't think she was such a little girl. We were two sweaty women on a couch, and it was getting late, and I told her I had to teach in the morning. She asked if she could stay over and I said yes, but she needed to stay in the guest room.

I reminded myself that I wanted to find a long-term relationship; I was too old to be messing around, even with a brilliant woman who spoke several languages. Moreover, I was never good at separating sex and love and admire those who can.

Abigail slithered under my covers at the crack of dawn and we held each other, and my morning was a blur of coffee and teaching and anxiety. Later that day she texted, said she had no doubt we had chemistry but the age difference might be too much. Still, she wanted to hang out, and we needed to be careful with our hearts.

In the big picture, nineteen years wasn't impossible, but when I looked at the smaller picture, the photo of us together on my phone—her smooth skin, little girl face and big head, against my crow's feet and worry lines, she looked so much younger. And why the hell did she go after me if she knew how old I was to begin with?

I cried on and off all day, perhaps because I didn't get much sleep the night before, or because I felt duped, or maybe because I mourned my youth—this was the first time age had been an issue in a relationship. After all, I have women friends who are with much older men and they are happily married, so might this be a gender issue?

Now I was in my fifties, and the last decade had snuck up on me. *Surprise! You're getting old!*

I ran into a colleague who'd been with her partner for ten years, a woman seventeen years younger. She said it was all a mindset and things were working out just fine. "But," she added, "sometimes people think she's my daughter. I don't bother to correct them anymore."

I talked to another friend who married a man twenty years younger—they'd been together for twenty years. She said he was the one with the health issues, that at seventy-five, she was fit as a fiddle. When the couple had gotten together, they taught at the same university. Her colleagues didn't believe her when she told them.

It was Halloween and Abigail sent me a picture of herself dressed as a bumblebee. She texted: "Can we hang out later?"

Of course she dressed as a bee; she had a stinger and she'd sting me again if I let her.

Then again, she was brilliant, funny, sexy and creative, and she'd only be in town for a short while. Maybe I shouldn't look at all relationships as potential marriage material. Was it possible for me to enjoy the moment? I loved talking about poetry and love and life with Abigail, and if something did happen, she'd be gone in a few weeks.

That evening Abigail held my hand and asked me to kiss her. I kissed her. We hugged. "I'm leaving in sixteen days," she said.

"You know we're playing with fire," I said. "Don't you?"

She squeezed my hand. "Can we spend that time together?"

"Like a contained fire," I said, "a controlled burn?" I caressed her neck, breathed in her rosemary-scented hair. "One of those fires intentionally ignited to clear the land and recycle nutrients?"

"That's exactly it," she said. She placed her hand on my heart, but I stepped back. A neighbor waved from the street, his beagle tugging him along.

We agreed to enjoy each other for the time she'd be in town.

As long as we set clear boundaries, I figured, we'd be okay, although contracts of the heart might be harder to abide by than, let's say, contracts with a home inspector.

I gave her the key to my house, and for the next sixteen days, we shared stories and food and poetry and our bodies and we relaxed into that contained field, burning and bright. On a daily basis, we strolled at a nearby lake, our hips snuggled, my dog romping by our side. We ate expensive pistachio ice cream in bed and watched videos on YouTube. One morning she showed me her online dating profile and asked if I'd respond, and I said I wouldn't have seen it in the first place—she was out of my age range.

Our contract worked, at least for the first week, although one morning I woke up sad; I felt part of a threesome, and Time was the other woman, my nemesis, my competition.

But if Time were the other woman, just then she gave me the option to enjoy, to *have at it*.

I heard that men date younger women because it makes them feel more boyish again. Abigail made me well aware of my age, especially when my gray roots started to show. I mentioned I needed to dye my hair. She went on about how she liked my gray roots and suggested I go all gray. I said I wasn't ready for that, not yet. She said, "I have a few white hairs," and I looked and looked and finally found one. And when she ordered a glass of wine at a local bar, she got carded, and that made me even more aware of our age difference.

I played my guitar and sang for Abigail, and she said her heart burst open when I scrunched up my face and grinned. And I took her to my gym and she used a worn-out bathing suit a friend had left at my house, a little too small and it drifted up her ass in the pool, and we laughed and laughed, and the lone man in the pool laughed along but had no clue why. And every day I pointed to the Japanese Maple, the reds and oranges lighting up the sky, the tips of the uppermost leaves starting to fray, and I'd say, "That's our tree."

I couldn't imagine that a year later, I'd be comforting her, as her friend, when the woman she would get involved with broke her heart over and over, how we both would look at our experience as a re-booting, but not without a price. It took several months of emotional untangling.

Yet, as a male friend said, "The Little Girl delivered."

Abigail and I went on "a proper date," as she insisted. We went to the Sky Bar, its patio overlooking the Blue Ridge Mountains.

She wore her slinky black dress and got carded, and it felt like porn when she flipped her leg onto mine, and we shared an apple cider froufrou drink. For a moment I felt like a middle-aged man with a prostitute. It didn't help that a gang of frat-looking boys were huddled in the corner. Abigail asked, "Are you okay with my leg like this." I told her I was, but really I wasn't. I never liked to call attention to myself, especially in front of frat boys. Yet there I was, in the place of discomfort, the place Abigail and I talked about, where the real learning happens, the place where I began to acknowledge my own aging process. From this place, I also learned I was still capable of attraction, of passion, of love, not only with others, but with my fifty-something body, and at times, even my graying hair.

Before Abigail drove off for good, we hugged and she wept and dabbed tears and snot with her jacket sleeve. Her car glided in reverse from my driveway, rolling over dried up leaves, leaves I would later compost into nutrients to feed next year's harvest. She put her car in drive, waved one last time, and stepped back into her life, and I into mine, a chorus of leaf blowers blasting in the distance.

MY FATHER'S MUG

LAST TIME I VISITED MY FATHER IN NEW YORK, the first thing he did was insist I take a coffee mug back home with me. "Take the cup," he said. "It's a beautiful cup!" He had donated money to a charity and received the mug as a thank you gift. Over and over he repeated himself: "It's a very nice cup!" Wheeling his walker behind me, he said, "You should take it!"

It's not unusual for my father to repeat himself. He's always been anxious and obsessive, and once he gets on a roll, he can't stop. In the past, his obsessions could be downright sadistic. When I was a shy teenager, he'd say, "What's wrong with you, why don't you have any friends?" He offered me five dollars to call a friend, knowing full well I had no friends to call.

I've since tried to humor him. But when he said it again: "You need to take the cup," I started to lose my patience.

"I only have a carry-on bag!" I said. "Besides, I have plenty of mugs at home."

"But it's a nice cup!" he said.

Finally, he maneuvered his way into an easy chair and picked up his iPAD to check the stock market.

My father's back is twisted and hunched over. He could barely walk. It breaks my heart to see him struggling like that. Yet while growing up, I was terrified of him. Every so often his face would turn beet red and he'd scream at me and my siblings and we'd hide in the back of closets, under beds, behind the dirty laundry.

Now he asks, "So how are you? What's going on with you?"

I never talk about my personal life with my father, especially my romantic life, although after meeting my college boyfriend, he did give me his assessment: "Good vocabulary, ugly as sin." Ten years later, he said: "Send grandma a recent photo of yourself. She wants to set you up with a police sergeant. He's Jewish."

My father looks up from his iPad and says, "How's that woman from Madison?"

Earlier in the year, I had told him about a girlfriend from Madison, although I didn't use the word *girlfriend*. But he knew. I even showed him pictures of us together. I mentioned her because my father grew up in Madison, and while I was there, I visited his childhood home—the home where his mother told him he wasn't smart enough to get into college, where his army colonel father called him a moron.

Now I look at the white-haired man in front of me.

Never the most supportive of parents, when I told my father about my upcoming trip to Mexico, he said, "You don't need to be going to Mexico and shitting all day long. Why don't you visit Epcot Village? You'd love it." When I got accepted to a Ph.D. program, he said, "Stop with the school already. Just get a job in an advertising agency." And when I mentioned I was reading Marx for a class, he said, "You don't need to be reading Marx. He was a filthy bastard who never took a bath."

During my first semester teaching a college class, a colleague wrote up a glowing teaching observation. I showed it to my father, figuring, since he worked as a schoolteacher, he would appreciate it, maybe even be proud of me. But instead, he looked up and said, "This is beautifully-written! Where did this woman go to school?"

My father taught middle school social studies in Queens, New York. Most of his students were African-American. One of my earliest memories—my father took me to his class the day after

Martin Luther King's assassination. He talked about the Civil Rights Movement and King's impact on it, and together he and his students sang "We Shall Overcome." A few students wiped tears from their faces.

On the morning of my departure, again my father said, "Take the cup! It's a very nice cup!" And so I took the cup.

I snapped a photo of him, a big grin on his face, holding up the mug. What I didn't say before—he donated money to the Human Rights Campaign, the largest national LGBTQ civil rights organization, and they sent him the mug as a thank you gift. It *is* a nice cup. It's a deep blue with HRC's equality logo embossed on it.

Before leaving for the airport, I bent down to hug my father. Finally I heard in my head, those words he could never say aloud: *I'm proud of you.*

ON DEATH *and* DYING (MY HAIR)

I WORKED WITH A WOMAN AT A SIGN COMPANY in New York City, and that's where we made those YOU ARE HERE fire exit maps placed near elevators. Both in our twenties, she went on about how gray hair is sexy on women, and I said, "If you think it's so sexy, then why don't you dye your hair gray?" I didn't think about going gray until I started to go gray, at thirty-eight, just a little bit by the temples. My hairdresser suggested I get a dye job, and I said okay. On my way back from the salon I got into my first car accident. It wasn't awful and the car was fixed and I ended up knowing the boyfriend of the woman who rammed into me. He drove me to the rent-a-car place and that night I met a woman with whom I would later have a tumultuous relationship—she had guns and liked to drink. Maybe the car accident and screwed up relationship should have been signs not to dye my hair again.

I didn't, not for three or four years, because my hair didn't have a lot of gray. Now if I don't dye it, I'd probably be pretty gray, although I don't know for sure. I don't go religiously to the hairdresser like some of my friends, every five or six weeks. Instead, I forget about it and then notice the gray roots sprouting up and I call the hairdresser, who is usually booked for the next three weeks, so I say *fuck it, I'll dye it myself*. So I buy that Clairol Basic Instinct stuff and do it myself, but that stuff doesn't last more than two weeks and, oh, it's not Basic Instinct, it's Natural Instinct. *Basic Instinct* was the movie starring Sharon Stone that came out in the early 90's. Stone played a bisexual murderous narcissistic psychopath who icepicks her lover to death. No wonder why gay activists criticized the film's portrayal of bisexuals. At the time it seemed that all lesbian characters in movies were portrayed as either drug addicts or murderers. You know, not very good role models for someone coming out, like me. Allie Sheedy in *High Art* and Gina Gershon in *Bound* were cute and all, but thank heavens we have better role models today, but don't most of them dye their hair? Take a look at Rachel Maddow, or Ellen DeGeneres, or David Sedaris. And then there's Anderson Cooper, son of Gloria Vanderbilt, who might dye his hair so it's one shade of silver. Maybe he's too rich and famous to care about going gray. Or maybe he's a man.

Is going bald for men akin to going gray for women? What about Donald Trump's comb-over? What if he went gray and showed his bald spot? At least men could shave their heads and look kind of hipster with a shaved head and facial hair. So what if Donald Trump looks ridiculous and he's with a woman, an immigrant, who doesn't speak perfect English, and he wants to build a wall and keep the immigrants out? Maybe it's not his comb-over that's the problem; maybe it's his attitudes about immigrants and women, how he said he would never change a diaper, that's what he pays his staff, probably immigrants, to do.

Are gray-haired women in their forties, fifties and sixties, who don't dye their hair, revolutionaries by default? By accepting their gray? Many have beautiful faces so we can look at them and say, wow, they are gray but they look fantastic.

Women who let their hair go gray are rebels, just as people who aren't on Facebook: by taking no action, they're making a statement.

I can see the sexiness in gray, but I also understand why we dye our hair in this age-phobic world. Never mind the cancerous chemicals that might take some years off our lives, or at least that's what evidence has shown. Yes, opting out of dying your hair is like opting out of Facebook. And we all know that Facebook makes you depressed, almost like watching television, so easy to get sucked in. You know, when you go to check the weather on your phone and forty-five minutes later you're watching videos of rescued dogs and old women tap-dancing and orange-faced monkeys getting their hair brushed. And then clicking on a link that gives you the twelve signs if you're dating a narcissist. And two hours later, your eyes are swollen from looking at the tiny screen. And that's enough to make you go gray. By the way, there is a Facebook page called: "Going Gray, Looking Great."

If you do get a dye job, you have to sit in the hair salon for two hours, under one of those stupid dryers reading *People* magazine, yet another article about Prince William and Princess Kate. And isn't *People* magazine like Facebook? They both make you feel bad about yourself for not being happy, rich and beautiful, and where are the gray-haired women in *People*? Women don't go gray in *People* magazine, and who the hell cares? They're certainly not *my* people.

I have to admit I did care about Princess Diana, maybe because we were from the same era, and she finally found love with the son of an Egyptian millionaire, and then bam, she was killed in a car accident.

Maybe if everyone went gray and got off of Facebook we'd all be happier, because isn't it about being okay with ourselves and accepting that we're all going to die? Like my college boyfriend, the anarchist, said, "Life is one long march to the tomb." And ain't that the truth. If people actually acknowledged they're going to die, wouldn't they be nicer to one another?

I found a few online articles about gray-haired women: "Seventeen Silver Vixens Who Will Have You Canceling Your Next Dye Job," "Six Reasons Gray Hair Is White Hot Again," "In case you didn't get the memo, gray hair is hot. And sexy! Just check out the silver foxes on the Red Carpet—Diane Keaton, Jamie Lee Curtis, and Helen Mirren." But can gray hair represent a stressed out life? According to an old legend—Marie Antoinette's hair *turned grey with stress and fear* the night before her execution. She is also the person often attributed with the statement: "Let them eat cake."

I've always been a little uptight about getting older, even at twenty-four and tried out for an all-girls band called the Tomboys. They were twenty-two, and they liked me at first, but when I practiced with them, I couldn't learn their songs fast enough. They called out the chord progressions and I'm really bad with following directions, even on the box of Basic Instinct hair dye. I leave the dye on for over twenty minutes because I figure it would last longer that way, but it still loses its zing in two weeks, and the longer I leave it on, the more deadly it is for my bloodstream. The irony of it all—while I try to keep myself looking young, I'm actually killing myself. Or am I just buying into our age-phobic society, the society that says if you're gray, you're old and washed up and the next step is death. Is dying our hair to cover up the gray a denial of death, a holding onto our youth? We all want to look good, especially on Facebook, and I make no judgments. Or maybe a little judgment—I dye my hair and I'm on Facebook, and I do think about aging and death, more so now that I'm getting older and realize I don't have all the time in the world. All the while, I do have the opportunity to be part of a hipper crowd of older women, as the title of a recent news article suggests: "Cougars, Gray Panthers, Silver Foxes: It's a Jungle Out There," and soon enough, I'll probably step into that jungle, a word originating from the Sanskrit word *jangala*, meaning uncultivated land, a wild land where we could roam without rules, where we could stretch and roar and swing our hips, where we can shake our wild gray manes with our sister cougars and foxes and panthers.

SLEEP CYCLES

1

SOMETIMES SLEEP, no matter what I do, never comes. Like when I crashed on a friend's couch in New York, a comfortable leather couch she found for free on Craigslist. I used earplugs, breathing techniques, but nothing helped. Six months later, my friend invited me to stay again. I said no. I didn't want to be near that couch. Three years later, my friend told me she invited a shaman to her apartment. "Get rid of it," the shaman said, pointing to the couch. "It's got negative entities living in it." Similar to lice, he said, entities like to jump to a fresh source of energy.

2

DESPERATE FOR MY MOTHER'S ATTENTION, I accompanied her on outings to antique shops, even though flapper dresses, Victorian furniture and sepia-toned postcards with faded script of people long dead frightened me. It didn't take long before I tugged at her coat and begged to leave. As if I had amnesia, I went with her again and again.

My mother sorted through stereoscopes and cast iron trivets, mesmerized in her own mothball paradise. She hummed and caressed carnival glass and washboards.

On a rickety porch, I waited outside and cried.

I never questioned why I felt out of sorts in antique shops. After all, I know people who fear wind, buttons, and flutes.

3

IN MY TEENAGE YEARS, I babysat on weekends. Late at night, too scared to watch old black and white movies, I opted for the only other choice on television—harness racing. I'd much prefer to watch horses trot around a brightly-lit track than subject myself to those now deceased actors.

4

MY THEORY ON WHY I'M UNCOMFORTABLE in antique shops is similar to why I have insomnia; maybe I have a thin skin when it comes to filtering out different energies, sounds and smells. Alternative healers might call this thin skin my aura. Rooted in Greek, the word *aura* means "breath," "cool breeze," "air in motion." Mystics view the aura as the essence of the individual, the subtle emanation surrounding the body of a living creature. In a cartoon version, Pigpen from Charlie Brown demonstrates this by the filthy aura frolicking around his body.

5

AT TIMES I'M SCARED I'LL DIE OF SLEEP DEPRIVATION. When my mind is like a prank birthday candle that won't go out. One night I began to read a well-researched book about sleep. In the preface, the author writes about how lack of sleep could lead to cancer, Alzheimer's disease and diabetes. Anxiety kicked in full throttle. I closed the book, donated it to Goodwill.

6

I MET A WRITER OF SURREALIST NOVELS, a billionaire's daughter, at an artist residency. "I wish I had insomnia," she said. "My favorite writers had insomnia: Kafka, Dickens, Nabokov. You're so lucky."

7

KERRY, A FRIEND IN GRAD SCHOOL, invited a handful of classmates to her mother's old Victorian house for a sleepover party; her mother had left town for the weekend. Somewhere in Upstate New York, the house had a cemetery in the back, headstones dating to the 18th century. We cooked dinner, danced, played music. I slept in her mother's bedroom, but an hour after falling asleep, a teenage girl wearing a tank top stood by the bed, arms crossed, dark straight hair down to her waist. She stared at me, hard and curious. "Hello?" I said.

I threw my head into a pillow and turned on the light. The girl disappeared. I got up, walked around. Everyone was sleeping. Was it a dream? In the morning, I told Kerry about the ghost.

"Really?" she said. "What did it look like?"

I described the teenage girl, the hair, the tank top, the blank expression on her face.

"Weird," Kerry said. "Six months ago, my fourteen-year old niece jumped in front of a train. She was close to my mother. My mother tells me she feels my niece's presence in the house and talks to her."

She showed me a snapshot of the same teenage girl, hair down to her waist, the girl who checked out a stranger sleeping in her aunt's bed. Although spooked and exhausted, I felt honored, a little special, to see into another world, to know the other world sees me.

8

AN ACUPUNCTURIST STUCK NEEDLES IN MY ANKLE, my ear, my hands and left the room. I closed my eyes, exhausted from lack of sleep, and saw my mother, her distant gaze, her freckles, red hair, the mole on her left cheek. Tears oozed. I didn't hold back, not until the acupuncturist plucked the needles out, as if sealing off a dam.

9

"I DON'T THINK I'M DEPRESSED," I told my therapist after I could barely sleep for two weeks. My school year had finished and I was on my way to Greece.

She didn't think I was depressed either. "Maybe you're used to worrying about something," she said, "and your brain has a void that needs to be filled."

My acupuncturist advised me to meditate.

My doctor, an older man about to retire, prescribed hormone replacement therapy. I didn't pick up the prescription; I didn't think my hormones were the problem.

But I drank whiskey, smoked weed, popped Melatonin and anti-anxiety medication. I moved my bed. Nothing worked. On a good night, I slept between two and four hours and woke up with a hangover.

I wondered if people could die of sleep deprivation. Apparently there are no known human cases of death caused by lack of sleep, but in the 1980's a University of Chicago researcher, Allan Rechtschaffen, conducted a series of experiments on rats. After 32 days of total sleep deprivation, all the rats were dead.

Two friends recommended shamans they knew. Both were booked up for a month.

Before flying to Greece, I visited my father in New York. I slept fine in his apartment, even on an old pullout couch with springs jabbing my back. I slept well in Greece. Now convinced my home was the problem, not my hormones, I had to do something. A friend recommended I call a psychic in Idaho. "She's the real deal," she said. The psychic told me I needed to purify my aura. She told me I needed to protect myself from negative energy, surround myself with light, have confidence, burn sage and white candles, chant OM, say prayers. "I keep hearing the words," she said, "*Purify your aura.*"

"It's easy enough," she said, "to tell the spirits to leave. They don't necessarily have bad intentions." *This is my home*, she told me to say. *I will take care of it. Now it's your time to leave. I don't want to hold you back from your spiritual growth. You have the freedom to cross over to the other side, and I wish you well.*

She told me that if I feel heavy energy in the room, loud clapping could break it up.

"Did your mother have red hair?" she asked, out of the blue.

"She was a natural red-head," I said.

"She wants you to explore all options," she said, "and do what she didn't do. Branch out. Make changes in your life."

That night I burned sage, told the spirits to leave. But at three in the morning, when I still couldn't sleep, I got up and screamed, "Get the fuck out of here! Leave me alone! Let me sleep!"

And I slept.

10

FOUR YEARS AFTER MY MOTHER'S DEATH, I was a fellow at an artist colony in Woodstock, New York, just down the road from where Bob Dylan once lived. In an old mansion, I lived with ten other artists, my first colony experience. But I could barely sleep. Two times during the first week, I woke up with a white face staring in my face. Both times I yelled, "Hello?" Once I turned the light on, I figured the white face was part of a recurrent dream. In the same week I had another dream: in my parents' bedroom, I told my mother about the white face waking me. She said she had also seen ghosts. She looked at the wall in front of her. Orbs of light danced around in a circle. My dream ended.

I told another resident, a painter, about the white face. The artist had dark hair down to her waist and drove an old turquoise Volvo. She pointed to the front left corner of my bedroom. "That's where it is," she said. "I definitely feel a presence."

She burned sage and frankincense and asked the presence to leave. Yet I didn't want to take a chance with meeting the white face again. I slept in my studio. And slept fine. The painter stayed for another month after I left. She asked the next occupant in that room about the presence. Without a pause, the new resident told her: "There's a ghost in the room. She's a nice ghost."

My friend said, "But the ghost kept my friend awake."

"Maybe," the new occupant said, "she's trying to remind her to think about her mother."

THE GRIEF BIRD

A SMALL PIECE OF MY GRIEF RESIDES IN LONDON, where I learned of my mother's sudden death. My acupuncturist said I'm holding onto mother-grief, that's why I can't sleep. She said grief gets trapped in the body, in the lungs in particular.

I usually fall asleep fine, but grief wakes me in the night, as if a trapped bird, its wings fluttering, banging against my lung's upper and lower lobes. When a child might scream at the "top of her lungs," when a mother runs to lull her back to sleep. As if I have a protector, I often sleep better next to a partner, a shield from outside fears and worries, but when I'm alone, anxiety takes over, when breath is constricted, when I throw my covers off and hold my ribs.

Psychologists say anxiety is your friend, your guidepost, if you listen to it, its roots from the German word "angst," meaning "narrow," referring to the narrowing of the bronchial passages. The lungs regulate the sweating process, enabling water vapor to ascend and scatter to the skin pores, controlling the skin, sweat glands and body hair. Along with anxiety, grief weakens the lungs, demonstrated by the heaving that occurs when crying. It's a fact that anxiety and grief can cause asthma, which my mother developed while pregnant with me. Although I didn't inherit her asthma, perhaps I inherited her grief. Inherited grief, transferable grief, like frequent flier miles.

Another piece of my grief might be walking the streets of Rome, the city where I woke from a nightmare of a burning car at precisely the same time my mother took her last breath, the city where an old man wiggled his tongue at me, where young men pressed up against me on crowded busses, where, as if he were an omen for what was to come, a man with a half-burnt face sat down next to me while I ate lunch in a park. I rose up slowly and ran, abandoning my sandwich and souvenir postcards from the Sistine Chapel.

I missed my mother's funeral. Maybe this is why most of my mother-grief has set up home in my lungs. I thought I'd find closure a year later, when my father drove my siblings and me and Grandma Becky to the cemetery, to the unveiling ceremony, where we removed a veil covering the headstone, a reminder of days when family members erected a monument themselves, where we said a prayer and left stones.

Even birds need closure. When a crow is struck and killed by a passing car, a convoy of companion crows descend and walk circles around the deceased for fifteen to twenty minutes—a roadside service so to speak. The magpie holds similar rituals. They've been known to place clips of grass alongside the departed bird.

Some say insomnia is a form of holding onto control, of not wanting to let go of consciousness. Might holding onto grief be a form of holding onto my mother? She wasn't the nurturing mother I had imagined mothers to be. Instead, she spent hours at the shopping mall, only to return most of her purchases the next day. In a recent dream, my mother was still alive but in a nursing home—the accident left her with a terrible brain injury. I walked around lower Manhattan with my father and asked him over and over where she was, but he wouldn't tell me. "Where is she?" I screamed. Finally he wrote the address down with a marker on a shiny sheet of paper. I couldn't make sense of what he wrote. I yelled, "Tell me where she is!" He said she was in a Jewish nursing home in Brooklyn. Maybe a piece of my grief lives in Brooklyn, the birthplace of my mother.

I used to be a great sleeper. I stayed in European youth hostels with forty or fifty to a room. At times, I'd wake up to the sounds of anonymous tooth-grinding or sleep-talking, but always fell back to sleep. Now when I wake up in the middle of the night, I read, or listen to a podcast. One night I listened to a podcast about a woman who felt a succession of heavy drips landing on her bed in the middle of the night. A leaking pipe, she thought, but later learned it was a dead man decomposing in the apartment above. I couldn't get back to sleep, thinking about the drip of death.

Somehow my body knew, from across the Atlantic, about my mother. Although asthma didn't kill her, two collapsed lungs as a result of the car crash did. During my childhood, my mother often wheezed and gasped for breath, asking one of the kids to find her inhaler. "Hurry," she whistled from her tightened throat. "I can't breathe."

"Be careful whom you love," Djuna Barnes writes in *Nightwood*, "—for a lover who dies...will take somewhat of you to the grave." Although my mother wasn't my lover, she took somewhat of me with her, and still a piece of her lives in me. The breakup with a recent ex, who wasn't my mother but was *a* mother, compounded my grief, making it my mother/lover grief. I didn't see that ex often because of her three children and the geographical distance between us. When she slept beside me, I slept well, but when we were apart, I stirred through the night with hot and cold sweats. *Perhaps it's that time of life*, I told myself, *when I'm supposed to have hot flashes and not sleep well.* Yet when we called it quits, my lungs opened wider. Maybe a piece of my grief lives in the Midwest, where I was born, where my father was born, where my mother's chest first tightened.

Similar to liberated Holocaust survivors who didn't know what to do when the gates opened, maybe my mother-grief, that trapped bird, is comfortable speaking the language of grief, the only language it knows well, despite the cage door wide open, like the survivors who stood there, paralyzed, comforted by confinement because that's all they knew.

I imagine the grief inside of me as a bruised-up bluebird, accustomed to waking in darkness and flailing about, the darkness that grieves for the mother I had and never had. And I picture the exhausted bluebird finally flying from the confines of its cage, falling into a deep slumber and waking in the quiet sun, like the sun had been there all along, its bluebird bruises transforming into the color of sky, blue on blue, until you can't tell the bird from the sky.

ON *the* BENEFITS *of* LIQUID SOAP

BEFORE TRAVELING TO THE WEST COAST for my book tour, I thought I'd do some rogue "marketing." Since I was single, why not invite women I met through online dating websites? I emailed women who sounded like they might read books: "Hey, I'll be reading from my new book at X bookstore and looking for interesting women to have coffee with while I'm in town." Pretty soon into my marketing campaign, I began an email exchange with Carrie, a sporty blonde veterinarian from Seattle. My marketing campaign slacked off. Because my school term ended and she was housebound with pneumonia, we had plenty of time to communicate.

We first connected over our love of dogs and our New York roots. Carrie told me her gut felt happy after our first Skype date. She told me the last woman she dated walked out on her when she went on about the benefits of liquid soap over bar soap. She told me she liked a clean bathroom and kitchen. She told me she had been in a long-term relationship that ended two years ago, or was it three? We watched movies, took naps and ate meals over Skype. We even had a dance party.

I imagined hugging Carrie, maybe for a minute, maybe two, perhaps gazing into her gray/blue eyes that went so well with her orange scrubs, the outfit she wore before leaving for work. We'd giggle like we did when we told each other stories, or when our dogs met over Skype. Her dog stared at the ceiling. My dog ran from the room.

I imagined moving across the country and making a life with Carrie. Didn't love conquer all?

After a month of Skyping on a daily basis, we finally met on a street corner near her apartment. Taller and leaner than I had imagined, she wore jeans that practically fell off her slender frame, and a "Running is My Happy Hour" t-shirt. She shook my hand, looked at the ground and talked, about the weather, her dog, the mold in her living room. She told me about brunch options, the café down the street, but they had loud music, or the cool art deco place with good food but was always crowded, or the diner with decent food and nice booths, and I fell into Reserved Lori, and Carrie wouldn't make eye contact and it wasn't like she could be disappointed in my appearance—she saw me, day in and day out, not like the pre-photo personal ad days when you took chances, and because the photos were decades old, you'd have to make conversation with a person you didn't expect when all you wanted to do was run. After a month of laughing and dancing and napping together, my heart sunk, just as it did when I was fifteen and finally met a boy I had been communicating with over the CB radio, and although he had a soothing voice and I had imagined him to be a cute boy with a bowl cut, in person he was obese and pimply faced and now, Carrie gazed in every direction but mine.

I ordered a dish that sounded good but turned out to be drippy eggs floating in tomato sauce. I couldn't eat it. Carrie offered me a piece of her bread with a cooked egg on it. We walked through a suburban neighborhood and she continued to talk, about her family, her job. Her wristwatch was set to three hours earlier. I asked why, and she said she wanted to be synced up to my time—maybe a sign that she did really like me.

Yet I still felt uneasy, insecure, the same feeling I had growing up, when my family talked over each other, and I didn't say much because why bother if no one would listen. She led me to her bare-walled apartment that felt more like a hotel suite. From the living room window, I could see a sliver of Lake Washington. She ran to shut her office door where piles and piles of papers covered her desk. She asked if I wanted anything. Besides a bottle of vodka and jar of peanut butter, she didn't have much in her refrigerator. "I hate grocery shopping," she said. In the corner of her spotless bathroom was a jumbo Lysol spray, and on her sink, a bottle of lavender liquid soap.

Carrie accompanied me to my reading. After a day of feeling dejected, at least the audience acknowledged me and laughed at my story. I sat back down and she touched my shoulder. "Up there," she whispered, "you were Confident Skype Lori."

I remained Confident Lori when conversing with audience members afterwards.

Still recovering from pneumonia, Carrie said, "I should go home, but let's go to dinner." She ordered two vodka drinks and now her foot touched mine. Maybe she needed to loosen up.

She drove me back to my friend's house and we got out of her car. She hugged me, the hug I imagined I'd get when we met, or maybe it was just a drunken hug. I asked if she wanted to see me again, and she said yes, of course. "I like you," she said, looked at me, held my hand and caressed it. We gave each other another long hug and she drove off.

My friend had been going through relationship hell with her live-in boyfriend, and while they argued, Carrie and I Skyped. She pointed the camera at her Yorkie, lounging on her leg. She asked if I wanted to see her the next day. I said, "Now you're the Skype Carrie. Maybe this is a Skype relationship," both of us more at ease with the computer screen in between us, a safety net, only our virtual hearts on the line.

When we met up again, Carrie talked and talked and wouldn't make eye contact. We walked around the lake, and again I slipped into Reserved Lori and by dinnertime, I said something about going back to my friend's house.

"I want you to stay," she said. "We could make dinner."

She asked me to help her make a grocery list. "Ever since the accident," she said, "I've had a hard time organizing anything."

"Accident?" I said.

"I was in a skiing accident," she said, "a couple years ago. Sustained a traumatic brain injury."

She couldn't work for a year, maybe two. Since then, she built up a freelance practice. She drove from clinic to clinic. "It's better," she said, "that I don't work with the same people day in and day out."

Carrie pushed the grocery cart, while I grabbed basic foods: cheese, bread, milk. In the soap aisle, I grabbed a three-pack of Ivory and threw it in the cart.

"Don't you need soap?" I said, barely containing my laughter.

"I don't use bars!" she said. "They're breeding grounds for bacteria!" She took the bars out of the cart. "I only use liquid soap. And I'm pretty well-stocked." She looked at me sideways, not sure why I was laughing.

She didn't remember telling me about her ex walking out on her when she went on about liquid soap. Now she laughed too. "You're a weird one," she said.

Maybe I was playing out my mother issues. The more my mother averted her eyes from me—to the television, to the dog, to the best deals at the mall—the more determined I was to make her look at me. And I was going to make Carrie look at me. We sat on her couch and she sipped vodka and threw a ball to her dog. I took her hand and she looked at it and brought it to her lips and kissed it. But still wouldn't look at me. "All right," she said. "We're here. Together."

"And?" I said. "Are you nervous?"

"A little," she said. "I'm dealing." She touched my leg.

I stroked her long spine. She leaned forward.

"That feels good," she said.

I continued to rub her spine. "You want a back massage?" I asked.

"Sure," she said. I suggested we go to her bed, where she lay on her belly and I caressed her back and she moaned, and now I was Confident Skype Lori and she was a scared bird. She apologized for how thin she was. I asked if she had lotion, and at first I picked up the liquid soap, but found the lotion and rubbed it around her back, her long thin neck and I told her not to apologize. Without warning, she rolled over and said, "Okay, let's kiss and get it over with."

Let's just say it was awkward and fumbly, and she was on target when she said, "I feel like I'm in high school."

"Maybe junior high," I said.

Eventually we held each other, and I stayed over, in her bed. She said she needed more time; she wasn't ready for sex. "No worries," I said, relieved to have little to no expectations of physical intimacy. Getting close, in person, shouldn't have to be such a struggle. We slept well. In the morning, I made coffee. She hadn't made herself coffee in years; she usually bought it at the café down the street, and what a concept, she said, coffee in bed. She made eggs and bacon. While rearranging my bag, a copy of *Ms.* magazine fell out. Carrie pointed at it. "What's that?" she asked.

"You don't know *Ms.*?" I said. "It's a feminist magazine. Started by people like Gloria Steinem."

"Gloria who?" she said. "I'm not a feminist."

"You don't know who Gloria Steinem is?" I said. How could I even spend another minute with someone who never heard of *Ms.*?

"These days," she said, "women and men have just as much opportunity to make it in the world. No one helped me out."

"You're serious?" I said, now standing up and gesturing with my arms out.

"You're a feminist?" she said. "A radical feminist?"

"Yes, I'm a feminist," I said. "And so are you!"

"I don't think so," she said.

I tried to explain in simple terms what feminism is, the dictionary definition: the belief that women and men should have equal rights and opportunities. I told her about a documentary she needed to watch that shows how women are portrayed in the media—in advertising, in movies, everywhere, as sex objects without brains.

A lesbian in her late forties, from New York, who never heard of *Ms.* or Gloria Steinem? How could that be? I brought up the notion of white privilege and male privilege, concepts that helped my students understand racism and sexism and the connection between the two. Carrie insisted she wasn't privileged. She worked hard for what she had. She went on and on about how feminism was no longer needed, and besides, most of her friends were men, it was easier that way, and why did feminists have to scream all the time and—"

I leaned over. "—The only way to shut you up," I said, "is to kiss you."

We kissed. She pulled away and said, "Kiss like a girl!"

The refrigerator motor kicked on, a siren wailed in the distance. I looked at her, shocked and disgusted, and said, "Why don't you kiss like a boy?" Did she mean I was too aggressive? I didn't shove my tongue down her throat, and in retrospect, she probably felt like she lost control. To be intimate in any way, even to make eye contact, I now suspected, Carrie needed alcohol.

I put my shoes on. "I need to take a walk," I said.

"What?" she said. "You're not leaving, are you?" She got up and hugged me.

"I just need to walk," I said. I called a friend but didn't tell her about the "kiss like a girl" comment; it was too embarrassing. I sat on a park bench and watched a bird fly from tree to tree and told my friend about the brain injury and how Carrie never heard of *Ms.*

"Certain injuries cause memory loss," my friend said. "There's no way she wouldn't have heard of Gloria Steinem otherwise." My friend also said that organizational tasks are difficult for people with brain injuries.

When I walked back into her apartment, Carrie hugged me and apologized for the "kiss like a girl" comment. "That was mean," she said.

I accepted her apology. She wanted to watch the feminist documentary, *Miss Representation*, I recommended. That evening, I drove up to a bookstore an hour north to be part of a literary reading. She watched the film and rested, trying to ward off a cough and cold.

"I see your point," she said. "I never noticed how blatantly sexist the world is." She looked up the filmmaker and found out she would be in town in a couple weeks to screen a new film. She bought tickets. "Too bad you won't be here to go with me."

Carrie asked me to stay with her while she did paperwork: billing, follow-ups, etc. "I just can't get it together," she said. She had to run to a few appointments and gave me her key. "Take Max for a walk if you want," she said.

That evening, we went out for pizza and watched a movie and held each other, and because she started sniffling, kissing was off-limits. While she worked, I picked up cold medicines and cough drops and lunch. She texted, "I miss you in a way I don't fully understand." We settled into each other in a bickering-old-married-couple kind of way.

On my fourth night in Seattle, I stayed with my friend. She drank and argued with her boyfriend; I Skyped with Carrie.

On my last day in Seattle, Carrie became more pale and sneezy. "If I were you," she said, "I wouldn't share a bed with me." But I did, figuring I had a robust immune system, yet it would catch up with me after I left. We ate Mexican food and drank margaritas and she held my hand and we danced and she looked me in the eye, and I figured this was the best she could do. After I packed my rental car, we hugged. Both of us cried. She said, "See, I can be a sap too."

I rolled the window down. She leaned in and said, "If you lived here, I'd want to date you."

She later texted *I miss you. Call me!* She was in a grocery store and said, "Please stay on the phone, I do better with someone with me." She ordered a rib-eye steak from the meat counter. The next day she left a message: she wanted me to help organize her day, but when I called back, she didn't pick up. Eight hours later, I texted: *Are you okay?* She was fine.

The last time we talked, a week later, she was in a laundromat down the street from her apartment. The laundromat in her complex was filthy and moldy, she said, and the one down the street was clean and had brand new front loaders, and by the way, she was using liquid detergent, not powder. "You could pre-treat stains," she said, "by pouring the liquid directly onto clothes, and powder doesn't dissolve well and could leave residue—"

"—Thank you for giving me a lesson on liquid detergent."

Although, like Carrie, I didn't fully understand our connection, I did understand that connections could have a short shelf life. We completely avoided the initial stages of a romance, usually full of passion and new discoveries; instead, we settled into a weary, later-phase of a relationship, where nothing seems quite right but no one's ready to call it quits. I needed more than that. And maybe I had enough of slipping into Reserved Lori while someone rambles on and on, of trying to catch the attention of someone who isn't capable of giving it, of living in a virtual fantasy because that way, I didn't have to open up my own heart. Besides, why would I want to engage with someone who argued about the benefits of liquid soap over bar soap? In truth, there's scientific evidence that liquid soap is no more effective than bar soap in killing bacteria, and liquid soap has a 25% larger ecological footprint, leaving behind plastic bottles and pump dispensers, unlike bar soap, which gets smaller and smaller, like the image of Carrie in my rear-view mirror after I drove away. She held her dog and stood stone-faced, staring in my direction, until she disappeared.

CHASING SQUIRRELS

"**D**ON'T YOU GET TIRED of going from one relationship to the next?" a friend asked. "You must be exhausted!"
I am. I'm also ashamed. Why haven't I been able to find a long-term partner by now? After all, I'm the common denominator.

Like many, I have a notion that if I find a healthy relationship, I'll be more content, less anxious and sleep better. But not everyone agrees. According to the set-point theory of happiness, a concept popularized by two psychologists in 2005, our level of subjective wellbeing is determined primarily by heredity and upbringing, and as a result, remains somewhat constant. It may change for a short time, in response to, say, marriage, or a death in the family, but then returns to its baseline level. Love won't make us happier in the long term, set-point theory states. But I don't accept that pessimistic view of the world, and thus, I continue my search.

For the past ten years, I haven't been able to maintain a romance for more than nine or ten months. I've gone into each full of optimism and hope, full of excitement that I finally met my person, the person who will hold my hand and help me breathe more easily through the bumpy and not so bumpy road ahead. Yet soon enough, the situation becomes unworkable—perhaps our emotional baggage as a team becomes too heavy, or our projections of each other wear off and the reality of who we are doesn't match with the fantasy we had. Or maybe my standards are too high. Or the timing was off. Or I'm too neurotic and anxious. I live in a small town and maybe I just haven't had the best of luck. I'm not pointing fingers and saying all my exes were nuts. Some are good friends. All I'm saying is we didn't make a good match.

Last week I asked my therapist what she thought my problem was.

"Give yourself a pat on the back," she said. "You know when it's not working, and you get out soon."

I nodded. Other couples hang in there, they keep trying, and eight or ten or fourteen years go by and they're still trying, or not trying but resigned to the situation. After all, there are children to contend with and bills to pay and houses to sell and move in and out of. Or there's a shared lease in New York or San Francisco and the chances of finding an affordable place for one are slim. Or the idea of going on Match.com or OkCupid or Tinder is too repulsive, more repulsive than living with, but not communicating with, a long-term partner, as if they were two cats who tired of hissing at each other and now quietly reside in separate sides of the house.

My single friends are also searching, some more proactively than others, to find their emergency contact. But are we really hardwired to find a mate, similar to my border collie/corgi's instinct to herd sheep? While visiting a friend's farm, my dog whipped her stout body and short legs towards three grazing donkeys, as if her life depended on it. She herded them in circles until I intercepted, grateful one of the donkeys didn't kick her in the head.

Perhaps it's all about societal pressure to find and keep a partner, and if we're single we feel like misfits, losers, unlovable. Yet according to evolutionary psychologist David M. Buss, humans are innately inclined toward non-monogamy. One theory suggests the brain is wired to seek out as many partners as possible. But other animals are known to bond for life. Red foxes form a monogamous pair, share their parental and hunting duties, and remain a couple until death.

If only I were a red fox.

When I meet a potential partner, I ask about her last long-term relationship. More times than not, she tells me she should have gotten out earlier, that the relationship was great for the first six months or two years but downhill for the next eight or ten. Often, to expedite the situation, one part of the couple has an affair. I ask, "Did you feel like you were under house arrest?" That's when I get a confused look. But soon enough, she laughs and says, "Yup. Self-imposed house arrest. I was so miserable I had to do *something*. I'm so much happier now."

I asked a friend, a two-time divorcé, what percentage of couples he thought weren't content with their situations. "Seventy percent," he said. At first I thought the number sounded high. But when I thought about the fifty percent divorce rate, and how some of the other fifty percent are miserable but don't get divorced—the number seemed more than reasonable. Another friend told me she didn't think she'd ever get married but said she's much happier now that she's married and has a child. Before she met her husband, she wasn't particularly interested in dating. She'd go for years without looking. And then someone would set her up on a date. She recalled going out to dinner with a boring rich doctor and ordering ninety-five dollars worth of sushi.

Some say I need to be content alone before I find happiness with a partner. I agree. A lot of things make me happy and the list doesn't need to include a romantic relationship. I don't expect anyone to save me from myself, and I've spent many months and years alone, and even more time feeling alone when I'd been in a miserable relationship. Maybe this is why I'm able to get out quicker.

A friend said, "Maybe if you give it a rest, love might find you." That friend hasn't had a relationship in years.

I'm not getting any younger and, like looking for a job, I believe you have to put yourself out there. No one's going to call and say, *Congratulations, we want to offer you the job*, if you don't first apply for it. Then again, a friend's home security system accidentally went off and a state trooper—a George Clooney look-a-like, knocked on her door. My friend had considered herself a lesbian until that point, yet they've been dating ever since.

My father spent three months alone between my mother's death and the next woman. He's been with her for over three decades, and I see how having a partner has made his life easier. He has someone to watch movies with, to go out to eat with, to go on vacation with.

When I asked him how they were doing, he said, "We're both creeping around. We're holding each other up." When I asked what made him happy, he said, "Getting a good night's sleep."

My father's spine is curled like a jagged comma. "My back is brittle. It's falling to pieces," he said. He needs a walker to get around. His wife is hard-of-hearing and rarely uses hearing aids, understandably since my father tends to ramble on about his latest obsession. My father and stepmother continue to creep around in their two-bedroom apartment, the television blaring, a grandfather clock chiming every fifteen minutes. "We're fading out," my father said.

At least they're fading out together.

And so I imagine finding a partner who I could travel with, someone with whom to share creativity and joy, someone who could offer a bowl a chicken soup if I'm sick and tired. Maybe I'm just looking for someone to creep around with.

I look at the set-point theory of happiness as if it were the average miles-per-gallon a car gets. Hybrids aside, most automobiles get better mileage on the highway than stop-and-start driving in the city. And, as far as relationships go, I've been a city girl, stopping and starting way too much, and if I were a car, I'd probably be pretty dinged up. But I'm keeping the faith that one day I'll pull onto the highway and stay a while, perhaps put the car into cruise control, and my happiness set-point will rise, and I'd put the pedal to the metal and play Steppenwolf's "Born to be Wild" and get my motor running.

Maybe the set-point only spikes when getting on the highway ramp, yet the hope is that a healthy union will bring the original set point up a few notches and remain there.

Relationships have been a source of joy but also pummeled me to the point where I could barely recognize myself. One woman didn't have to do anything. Just her presence brought out a profound sadness in me. Perhaps she reminded me of my mother, lost in a world of hoarding, humming and shopping. Although this ex didn't hoard or shop excessively, when apart, I slipped off her radar. She'd forget about plans we made; she'd forget to call.

Now that I think of it, maybe I'm happier being single. Or being single and holding onto the illusion that love is out there and might make me happier.

In the meantime, studies show that practicing kindness may increase one's happiness set-point. Another way to raise the set-point is to have a project to go back to, to be in the flow—whether as a painter dabbing a brush stroke onto a canvas, or a nomad searching for love.

My dog has taught me a lot about happiness, about living in the moment. When I clip on her leash and tell her we're going to the lake, she cries and runs around and jumps and smiles and sticks her head out the car window. At the lake she wags her tail and makes eye contact with every passerby. Given her large border collie head, long and stout body, and squat legs, her unusual proportions cause people to say, "She looks like a comic strip character! As if her head was grafted onto the wrong body!" Others call her Yoda because of her big ears. I call her my ambassador of love. When she smiles, whoever looks at her smiles back, and that makes me smile too. Even if someone looks miserable and is walking off steam, they too crack a smile.

And then there are the squirrels. My dog instinctively chases them, knowing full well she'll never catch one. How could she think she would after fourteen years of trying? And if she did, would she know what to do?

Would I?

THE SCENT *of* NAG CHAMPA

JANICE NEEDED TO GET OFF THE PHONE. She needed to sit in silence. A minute before, I had told her about my plans to meet up with a friend, a friend I'd known for twelve years, a friend who happened to be single. I tried to explain we'd only ever been friends.

"I have to meditate!" she yelled. "You have fun with your friend!"

"Why are you so threatened?" I asked, gripping my phone, now in full throttle defense mode.

"You know how I feel about her!" she said. "I'm off to my meditation room."

Before I could eek out another word, the line fell silent.

I rarely drink, and if I have more than two drinks, I feel sick, but now I downed a shot of scotch to calm myself. And imagined Janice, sitting cross-legged, praying to a framed photo of a blissed-out Indian guru. It had been a year since she quit drinking and took up intense meditation, but I wondered if she had traded in alcohol for her guru.

All the while, I remained addicted to addicts of some sort, those who couldn't give me what I needed, those who I steadfastly defended myself to, those whose behaviors made me feel out of control, as if my words would somehow knock sense into them. Like I'd done in the past, I tried to understand Janice's situation. After all, her last two girlfriends cheated on her; once she felt more secure, she'd loosen up and trust. Besides the scotch taking the edge off, at least I had my dog, Belly, lying near me. She didn't mind when I pet other dogs.

Tall, lean and blonde, attractive in a pixie-ish kind of way, Janice had a bounce in her step and an impish smile. So far, we'd spent three weekends together, and for a moment, maybe two, I thought I had met my person. She was my age, a successful filmmaker, meditated every morning, went to kickboxing classes, and seriously considered a move to my small city from her hometown of Atlanta.

In the hotel parking lot where we had first met in person (we found each other on match.com), a mile from my home, her eyes veered down and shoulders hunched. Her limp handshake felt like a sweaty rag. On our way to a bar, she said, "If you're not attracted to me, I could leave tomorrow."

"Let's get to know each other," I said. "How was your drive?" Maybe, if I were on her turf, I'd be just as insecure.

By the end of the next evening, she loosened up, and we kissed and she showed me clips of her latest film. We held hands while watching Hillary Clinton's acceptance speech at the Democratic National Convention.

She brought homemade chicken treats for my dog. She loved dogs, and in fact, adopted two incontinent beagles that wore doggie diapers. As a testament to her love of animals, she told me a good chunk of her estate would go to a local animal shelter.

The second time she visited, she looked at artwork I created in my twenties and early thirties, mixed media photographs. She asked how I made them, encouraged me to take up art again. "I could help you get a show," she said. She also didn't understand why I made little to no money on my writing.

When Janice's accusations knotted up my neck, when she accused me of sleeping with my friends, why couldn't I find the strength I had over thirty years before, when I navigated

Manhattan's East Village with a don't-fuck-with-me-or-I'll-kick-the-shit-out-of-you attitude? Why couldn't I take control of myself, like I did when a clean-cut young couple stopped me on St. Mark's Place and asked if they could walk with me? I said, "Sure, as long as you're not a Moonie, as long as I don't have to take a free personality test and read *Dianetics*, as long as I could have control over my bladder," and they said, "Some people are so cynical."

I prided myself on cynicism, way too smart to ever join a cult, or even watch television, claiming that TV is a tool to control the masses, like religion.

On FaceTime, three hours after hanging up on me, Janice transformed into her sweet self, her impish smile lighting up the screen. She showed me her dogs curled up together. "Can't wait to curl up with you," she said.

The next time Janice visited, we met up with an acquaintance of hers, another filmmaker. He took pictures of us together, arm in arm. On the forty-five minute drive home, Janice's glazed eyes stared out the window, as if she were possessed.

"Anything the matter?" I asked.

"No," she mumbled.

This wasn't a comfortable silence. "You sure?"

"Fine," she said, her eyes affixed to the passing cement factory.

I'd much rather be alone than trapped in a car with a woman who claimed to be spiritual but disappeared and reappeared, as if drifting in and out of consciousness. Maybe she was thinking about her guru, or maybe in her head she'd been chanting.

Janice snapped back to her fun self, as if she stepped out of a gargoyle costume.

"Thanks for always making the drive here," I said.

"I like Asheville," she said. "And your dog is sick."

She looked at her phone after it dinged. She told me her ex was stalking her. "It's like she knows what's going on with me," she said.

"I hadn't heard from her in almost a year, and during the last two weeks, she won't stop texting me." She told me her ex has guns. She told me she once had to pull a gun away from her ex after her ex threated to kill herself.

"Maybe it's best I don't visit," I said.

She took my hand and twirled me around the kitchen, her beaded necklace slapping against her neck, the beads that she claimed protected her. "They're dried seeds from the Himalayan mountain range," she said. She showed me the website where she got them, a website run by the Indian guru she followed.

"A hundred and twenty-five dollars for beads?" I said.

"Every necklace is blessed," she said. "It's well worth the protection."

The website also advertised expensive jewelry, yoga mats and incense burners. "You sure you're not involved in a cult?" I asked.

Janice's blank expression appeared. Then disappeared. "Not at all," she said. "He's amazing."

A friend of mine had gotten involved in a cult while in college. For three years, she wasn't able to speak to her family and friends, worked fifteen-hour days for no money and barely slept. Her family hired a deprogrammer and eventually she worked for the deprogrammer. She knew that Janice's guru was considered a cult leader. She told me cult leaders are often seen as special individuals with unusual connections to God. Members of the organization show great attention and love to new members, and those who do not keep in step with group policies are shunned. Also, members are shunned for having contact with others outside the group.

Now that I think of it, for the price of affection and momentary pleasure, I have given up friendships, didn't take care of myself, allowed anxiety to take over my body, lost sleep, my appetite, and control. I swigged alcohol even though it made me sick, but for the moment, it calmed me, like it used to calm Janice, until she blacked out, until she didn't remember what happened the night before, until she hit rock bottom and almost died in a car wreck. Like cult members, I could have stepped away at any time. But affection and pleasure are hard to step away from, especially when I had a beaten down sense of self-worth, as if I didn't deserve more than crumbs, as if there was nowhere else to go but off a cliff.

Because of Janice's emotional hold on me, because of the initial intoxicated sensation I got from her attention—and wanting that back, I might as well have been wearing the beaded necklace and praying to a framed photo of a guru in white.

Two days after Janice left, she was enraged. I took too long to answer a text. "I kept checking," she said.

I told her I didn't have my phone with me when I walked Belly. "When I got back home," I said, "a friend called."

"What friend?" she said. "How do you know her?"

I told Janice I met my artist friend on a dating website four years before and we'd only ever been friends. "She likes butch women!" I said.

Janice, again, said she needed to get off the phone and meditate.

I barely slept. And thought about the many relationships I'd had, the many nights I couldn't sleep, especially with partners I didn't trust: the one who bought me a computer and fleece jackets and a vacation to Puerto Rico but screamed at me, then ignored me, after I tenderly brushed a crumb off her face; the one who showed up an hour late and drunk to a concert. When I expressed my disappointment, she said, "I bought those tickets, and *you're* complaining?" Over and over I tolerated bad behavior and accusations, defended myself against them, or quietly internalized them, like my mother did. She stared off in the distance and hummed when my father screamed at her.

The next time Janice visited, she rushed into my house. She drove without a break, pecked me on the lips and ran to my bathroom to pee. She hadn't yet noticed the incense smell saturating my home, incense I didn't burn. "It's strange," I said, after hugging her. "I was on the phone when I started smelling it. I thought something was on fire." Belly sniffed Janice's low-cut black leather boots and halfheartedly jumped to greet her.

Janice stepped lightly through my living room, her nose sniffing and twitching. "That's Nag Champa. I *hate* that smell." She turned around and asked, "You sure you didn't burn any incense?"

I assured her I hadn't burned incense for months and never even heard of Nag Champa. "I went swimming," I said, "and called my friend Cindy when I got home."

Now Janice's face snarled, hands in her back pockets. "Who the hell is Cindy?"

"The artist in Boston," I said. "I told you about her. Remember?"

"I can't remember all your friends' names," she said. "You sure you didn't burn any incense?" She shook her head. "Nag Champa reminds me of dirty hippies."

"I told you," I said, losing the little enthusiasm I had for her. "I was on the phone when I starting smelling it."

"I hate that smell," she said.

I told my deprogrammer friend about the Nag Champa smell in my house. "You probably think I'm nuts," I said, "but I did a Google search and found someone else who had the same experience. He wrote: *I smell Nag Champa when a particular guide of mine is around...and it's happened where others can smell it too.*" I didn't tell my friend that I thought my spirit guide might have been my mother.

She told me about crying uncontrollably after her mother died. And then feeling a warm sensation around her body. She saw her mother's face. She stopped crying. She said, "I'm a believer that there's something out there."

My friend said that Nag Champa incense is connected to an Indian Guru, Sai Baba—a self-proclaimed reincarnation of God on

Earth. He died in 2011. Along with the supposed ability to manifest holy ash as well as watches, rings and necklaces out of thin air as gifts for his followers, decades worth of allegations of sexual abuse and pedophilia were lodged against him. He left an estate worth over nine billion dollars. But his organization did a lot of humanitarian work—they opened hospitals and schools and provided drinking water to poor parts of India.

And his organization, or at least his incense, did me a service too. Over lunch, I said to Janice, "Maybe the incense is a sign."

"A sign for what?" Her lips puffed out.

I wanted to tell her this was a sign for her to *get out*. Of my house. My life. But instead, I said, "A sign to take Belly for a walk."

A week later, Janice learned her weekend retreat had been cancelled. She offered to visit. But I didn't want her to visit. She said, "But I really want to see you. I miss you!"

I said okay, come. But my gut hurt. My gut said you deserve better. My gut said you should be able to tell Janice you had gone to a yoga class that morning with your (single lesbian) friend, but for the sake of keeping the peace, you told her you went alone. My gut asked why the hell do you put up with her accusations and moodiness, and what the hell are you getting out of all of it? My gut said call her back and tell her to turn around.

And I called her back. "Look," I said, "it's best you don't come. I need to go."

And I got out. And didn't fall off a cliff.

But I did burn old pine incense I had in my kitchen drawer. Incense is used as a purification ritual in a number of religions to welcome God's visit. Whether my spirit guide, my guardian angel, my dead mother—whomever or whatever was responsible—I took it as a sign to leave Janice, to acknowledge that the only person I could change is myself, to purify my home, my body, my mind, a sign to let my own God in.

THREE VETERINARIANS

In the veterinarian's waiting room, a woman with a salt and pepper Cleopatra haircut held an old shaky poodle on her lap, one of its eyes sewn shut. "I can't do this anymore," she said, her eye shadow the same shade as her blue blazer.

"What do you mean?" I said.

"I won't get another dog after him," she said, caressing her dog's head. "Dogs die too soon."

A vet tech escorted the woman and her dog to a back room. Now I was alone with Belly, my trembling fourteen year-old dog. Upon the recommendation of the last woman I dated, I scheduled an ultrasound because of my dog's high liver enzymes. I didn't understand the medical terminology, but a number of vets had tried to explain the specifics to me, including the last three women I had dated over the course of a year—all of whom happened to be veterinarians.

I held Belly's quivering body next to mine and thought about the woman's comment. How many months, weeks or years would constitute living long enough to make pet ownership, or any kind of love, worthwhile?

Irises and bluebells were in full bloom when I met Vet Number One on match.com. We talked every day for four weeks before I flew across the country to meet her, where I already had plans to visit friends. When she saw Belly over Skype, she said she'd never seen such a beautiful dog: "Take that as a compliment from a veterinarian."

We talked while we drove to and from work. We talked every night. We texted sweet messages throughout the day. Too caught up in our email and Skype connection, I didn't think twice about the geographical distance between us. She studied Belly's annual blood-work and said I shouldn't be too concerned, even though a new vet at my clinic advised me to give her two different pills to bring the liver enzyme numbers down. Because Belly still looked and acted like a puppy, had a healthy appetite and loved her walks, I figured she was fine.

In person, Vet Number One only made eye contact when she was drunk. We spent four evenings together—dining, dancing, and bickering about her conservative viewpoints compared to my liberal ones. Clearly I couldn't be with someone who had alcohol and intimacy issues, but upon my departure, we hugged and cried. Maybe I cried for what could have been, the fantasy I created in my head. Yet as long as she lived across the country, as long as she had enough alcohol to buffer her heart, I didn't have to worry about mine.

And for the time being, I didn't worry about Belly.

Yet Vet Number Two, alarmed by Belly's blood-work, recommended that Belly get a bile acid test. I told my regular vet, Dr. Gold, about Vet Number Two's recommendation. He advised me to give Belly the two pills his colleague had recommended and he'd re-test her blood in a month. Belly continued to smile and waddle when we took walks, and she loved to greet other dogs.

The summer sun lit up the sky into the late evening when I had met Vet Number Two at my book reading, in her city, five states away from mine. We flirted and she joined me for dinner, where she told me about her bevy of children and other lovers. Over the course of four months, we spent five extended weekends together. The screaming kids, unanswered texts leaving me wondering if I was important, and most importantly, her need to keep the relationship open, took a toll on both of us.

As a child, when asked what I wanted to be when I grew up, I said a veterinarian but didn't know of any female doctors, not even on television. My mother encouraged me to be a nurse or a teacher. I hated dolls but loved stuffed animals. My sister had Barbie dolls, and I let my black poodle, Cindy, chew their heads off.

By eighth grade, my dream of becoming a veterinarian had been overshadowed by my love of photography and film. Besides, I hated needles and blood and dissecting frogs. Instead, I took pictures and wrote songs about Cindy, the only family member I could hold and hug. At thirteen, I bought a tiny white poodle with my own money and named her Sunshine—my constant companion in a town of mean girls who made fun of my fake Frye boots.

I had to leave my white pocket poodle behind when I left for college. A year later, she ran away from my mother. I felt incredible guilt for abandoning her. Over twenty years later I was ready to be a dog mom again and adopted Belly from the local humane society. I drove her five-pound body home in a shoebox, her big eyes staring at the world beyond the shelter cage. I took her to a vet—a short, rotund man who didn't make eye contact. Maybe it's true what I heard about vets: they relate better to animals than they do to people. Maybe, at times, I do too.

Two months after breaking things off with Vet Number Two, I met Vet Number Three on OkCupid. Maybe the third would be the charm. A Buddhist who liked to mountain bike, she lived two hours away. I cracked up when she told me about one of her clients—a Yogi dressed in white who let his cat wander in her waiting room. He opened his mouth wide and showed her his rotting teeth and wanted advice about them. She told him she only dealt in animal dentistry. She put crowns on police dogs and once did a root canal on a jaguar.

On her way through Asheville, we met for lunch and a walk on an icy day in December. I liked her but didn't think I liked her like that. Yet when I saw her checking out Belly's teeth, something in me shifted.

I drove two hours to visit Vet Number Three "as a friend." I stayed in her guest room and couldn't sleep, not a wink. Her ex of seven years, she later told me, left bad energy in the house. No one could sleep well in that room. She had two little dogs: one with three legs, the other that would whine if we made eye contact. At two in the morning, Belly cried; her body got stuck in Vet Number Three's dog door.

Despite the evil spirit in her home, Vet Number Three and I made a go of it, not just because she was a vet, although she definitely got girlfriend points for that. Soon into the relationship, I discovered that when I was out of sight, I was out of mind. She wasn't good at texting or talking. That wouldn't work for a long-distance relationship. Even she admitted, "It's what makes me a good surgeon. I'm hyper-focused on what's in front of me."

Vet Number Three, after studying Belly's updated blood-work, suggested an ultrasound, so there I was in the veterinarian's waiting room, sitting across from the woman with the poodle who said she couldn't do this anymore. Even though Vet Number Three and I had broken up a month before, we talked often, more often than when we were girlfriends.

Dr. Gold knew Vet Number Three from years ago—they did their veterinary residencies together. After he explained the ultrasound results that showed a prominent mass in Belly's liver, he offered to discuss my options with Vet Number Three. I could see Belly's long curved spine and big heart, the heart that connected to mine when, a decade prior, she had disappeared for a week while a friend watched her. A pet psychic had told me to connect our hearts with an imaginary "golden cord." I did, and Belly showed up at my friend's house thirty minutes later.

"It would be a major surgery to remove the mass," Vet Number Three said, "but Dr. Gold told me he'd get the surgery done if Belly were his dog." Even though I earned enough money to afford the operation, she offered to help pay for it. Maybe she thought that helping to offset the cost would be the deciding factor, since animal dentistry paid a lot more than teaching college.

I told her it was a kind gesture but wanted to think about it. Belly was almost fifteen and had arthritis. There were no guarantees the operation would be successful.

Now more concerned about Belly's quality of life than taking the risk of putting her through a major surgery, I wanted to show her the best time possible, so the three of us—Vet Number Three, Belly and me—met up in a coastal town four hours away. Belly romped on the beach and people still stopped and asked if she was a puppy, even though her hair was thinning and blotchy in parts.

A month later, I took her back to the vet's office to get an x-ray, to see if the mass spread. Still contained to one lobe, the dark form might have gotten bigger. Over the next two months, Belly's appetite became more refined until she only swallowed her pain pills with pâté. On a night she could barely sit because of her bloated stomach, I woke up at two in the morning to her bulging eyes staring me down. I tried to give her a pain pill, but she wouldn't eat it. It was time. I drove to the twenty-four hour vet clinic. Belly stood on the window armrest and sniffed the air. While waiting for a doctor to come in the room, I checked my phone. I hadn't heard from Vet Number Three in a few weeks, but she emailed a minute before: *How are you? How is Belly?* I told her I was saying my goodbyes at an all-night clinic and asked what she was doing up at that hour. She said she drank green tea and forgot it had caffeine and got up to do work and thought of me. The next day, she sent flowers, chocolate-covered strawberries and a Mary Oliver poem, and it hit me—Belly was gone. I was alone, really alone in my house for the first time in almost fifteen years. I curled up into a fetal position, cried and slept. When I woke, though, I didn't think about dogs dying too soon. Instead, I grieved for Belly, her unconditional love, and even caught myself listening for her tapping paws on hardwood floors.

A week after her passing, on my birthday, I held a ceremony to honor Belly's life. The autumn leaves began to turn. Thirty guests came over: friends, colleagues, and a handful of former students who had dog-sat Belly. I burned sage and we all told stories about her. A friend said, "I watched Belly one night and she slept in bed with me. It was my only lesbian experience." Another friend responded, "You could have done a lot worse."

And I could have done a lot worse than dating three veterinarians over the course of a year. It's not like I hung around veterinary conventions trying to meet veterinarians. I just happened to meet three vets in a row during the last year of Belly's life. Although three attempts at a long-term romance took a toll on me, it would take another two years to understand that dating emotionally (and physically) unavailable women, most likely, meant I was unavailable too. Yet the dynamic of yearning for unattainable love felt familiar, safe. And finally, after I said goodbye to a woman who easily swigged down a six-pack of beer in one sitting, I could say: *I can't do this anymore. It's just too painful.*

Maybe the vets I dated didn't make the best eye contact, and maybe my (false) hopes about each one died too soon, and maybe Belly died too soon, and maybe we all die too soon, but what is this life about, if not to connect with one another, and what are we to do in the meantime between bouts of love and grief?

HOLDING SPACE

I DIDN'T WANT BARB STORING HER CRAP IN MY GARAGE. But I couldn't come out and tell her. So I said I didn't feel comfortable having her unload boxes when I was out of town. Sure, I had a lot of space to spare, but that was my business. Besides the gardening tools, shovels and cans of paint, my old darkroom supplies lined the aluminum shelves—the enlarger I bought at thirteen, the glow-in-the-dark timer, the easels and trays I used to print black and white photos. In the laundry room of my childhood home, I had spent hours burning and dodging and developing photos, a place where I found solace, away from my mother, who'd barge into my bedroom and ask why I didn't have friends.

Although I had no intention of setting up a darkroom, I held onto the photo equipment; it reminded me of a safe space, where I could explore and create. And maybe I clung onto my dying friendship with Barb because I heard that little voice in my head, the voice of my mother asking what was wrong with me.

"I have your house-key," Barb said. "Can you give me your pet-sitter's number? I'll let her know I'm coming."

"Can you wait two weeks," I said, now exasperated, "until I get back?"

Five years before, I had considered Barb a good buddy, despite our differences. She grew up Southern Baptist. I grew up a New York

Jew. In our small North Carolina city, we found commonalities as single lesbian dog-owners and musicians. We talked multiple times a day on the phone, took vacations together, met for meals often. We watched each other's dogs and watered each other's plants. And during a difficult time I had with a home renovation, when other friends defended a depressed carpenter I had hired, Barb shot them down. She saw how he ignored me, talked to me with contempt.

Yet since Barb found a new girlfriend, she disappeared. I'd see her every now and then, usually when her girlfriend traveled for business, and more times than not, she'd complain about her. The last time we hung out, I invited Barb to dinner with my friend who introduced us to her new girlfriend. Afterwards, Barb said I asked too many questions.

Shocked at her accusation, I asked what was wrong with asking questions. Over the course of the evening, I asked the new girlfriend questions about her work, home city, nothing too personal.

Before Barb answered, I said, "Perhaps, here in the South, you take asking questions as invasive; yet where I'm from, asking questions shows that you're curious, that you're interested in learning about someone."

She apologized.

Barb and her partner could afford to pay for a storage unit. But my garage was convenient. They bought a house up the hill, a million dollar home with giant picture windows. And little storage space.

Barb said, "It would really help now if we can store a few things."

Unlike my childhood home, where our two-car garage was piled to the ceiling with junk my mother refused to part with, my garage was palatial.

"Let me think about it," I said.

"We'd really appreciate it," she said.

Barb called the next day and I relented. "I'll give you a month," I said. "That means you have to get your stuff out by August 1st."

"Great," she said. "We can do that."

Barb left boxes and boxes and ski poles and a paper shredder and a set of dumbbells and lamps in the corner of my garage. Her stuff weighed on me, and because she had my key, she came and went, taking things out, putting things in, as if it were her own personal storage unit.

Garage comes from Old French *varer*, meaning "to protect against," probably borrowed from Old Norse *vara*, "to warn," and *varask*, "to be on one's guard." I tried to guard my space, but Barb's boxes, ski poles and halogen lamps nagged at me. The extra junk in my basement became a warning sign, not only of a doomed friendship, but of my need for firmer boundaries. A *doormat*. A place to wipe mud off shoes and walk over. I was a doormat.

Barb called to let me know of her comings and goings, yet one morning, I woke to the rumbling garage door opening below my bed. My phone ringer was off.

I came downstairs to find her rummaging through a box. "Next week is August 1st," I said.

"I know!" she said. "You're so neurotic!"

We didn't exchange another word, not until August 1st, when she phoned. She said she arranged for a consignment shop to pick everything up. Two weeks went by. Now she said her nieces would rent a truck and take everything. And they did. Before leaving, she offered me her paper shredder.

She cleared out the basement and our friendship.

It would have been the death of our friendship, I had thought, if I didn't let Barb store her stuff. But how could you kill something already dead?

My therapist asked what I learned from the experience.

"It's not my job," I said, "to take on other people's crap."

I've since donated my darkroom equipment to Goodwill but kept the shredder. I gathered piles of bank statements and health records and fed them into the machine, which whirred and shredded, but soon into the growing confetti mound, a heap of paper got stuck in the shredder's teeth, and the motor moaned and whimpered before it came to a dead halt, before I placed the shredder in a big green trash bin and wheeled it to the curb, before a garbage truck unloaded it and left the bin empty, its flap down, an empty hollow in waiting.

BIG GUTS / BIG HEARTS

IF I STEPPED TOWARDS the majestic brown stallion trotting towards me, I figured he'd move away. I'd show *him* who was boss by puffing up my shoulders and maintaining my pace forward. But Zorro persisted. And I ran out of his way.

On her horse farm in the mountains of Western North Carolina, my friend Kim, practicing to be an Equine Facilitator, said, "You could have used your hands to push him away."

I never would have thought to shove a twelve-hundred-pound horse out of my way. It didn't help that I'd barely slept the night before. Like a ghost floating through the dusty corral, I felt vulnerable and weak. But once Zorro had bee-lined in my direction, I behaved as if I had my wits about me, as if I were in control.

When Kim had asked for volunteers to practice on—she needed to accrue a certain number of hours before receiving her Equine Facilitated Learning Certification—I jumped at the chance. I always looked at horses as beautiful and mysterious creatures. As a child, I fed them apples through a fence at the state fair, and once, a bucked-tooth teenager helped me hoist my body onto a pony and led me around a corral.

"By learning how to communicate with horses," Kim had explained the morning of the workshop, "we acquire skills that help our confidence, and improve our ability to connect with others." That day I learned that horses have big guts and big hearts, about nine times the size of a human heart. Their primary instinct is awareness. In the wild, they're prey animals to wolves, grizzly bears and mountain lions, so their survival depends upon reading their environment for signs of danger. They sense incongruities and act out, for example, when someone pretends that everything is fine but on the inside they're seething. In other words, horses are emotional mirrors. Incongruities signal danger. Each horse reacts differently, depending on their personality and role in the herd. An alpha mare may move towards the incongruity and check it out. Others may turn away.

When I stepped towards Zorro, he probably sensed how sleep deprived and out of control I felt, all because of a beady-eyed, charismatic colleague—Dr. D, who I had once considered a friend. His office, two doors down from mine, had enabled us to spend time talking about our lives. Even though he was married, he said he had been with men, and he and his wife were bisexual. I admired his openness. He laughed at my jokes and loved my writing. He invited me into his office and closed the door and gossiped about colleagues and students, and I found myself indulging with him. Afterwards, I felt sullied, like I had to wash off our interactions. Dr. D also charmed colleagues and students by joking with them, telling them how brilliant they were, and at one department party, wrestling on his front lawn with a male student. One night, following a panel discussion I organized at school, Dr. D laughed with two students in the lobby. One of the students invited me to join her and her friend and Dr. D for pizza. Dr. D looked away, making it clear he didn't want me there. My gut hurt, told me that Dr. D wasn't really a friend, but screw it, I had asked him to be part of the panel, and I was hungry, and those were my students too.

Yet Dr. D continued to charm me at school, and when it came time to recommend him to teach with me during a three-week study-abroad program, I gave him the highest endorsement. Because I had taught in the program the year before and was slated to teach in it again, my recommendation carried weight. I'd teach an arts class, and he'd teach a humanities class to the same set of students. "We're going to have so much fun!" he said when he learned he secured the job. That evening, I invited him to a holiday party at my house, but he said his wife needed to rest. For the two years I'd known him up to that point, we had never spent time together outside of school or school events.

In London, we lived in an on-campus apartment; the students lived nearby in a dorm. To my horror, during the second night, he encouraged students to drink, gamble at a video casino, and get stoned with him. I refused to engage. On the third day, after his session, he passed me in the hallway of our apartment. "By the way," he said, "I told the class you were a lesbian."

I caught my breath. "Don't you think that should have been my choice to make?"

"Everyone knows about you," he said.

A week into the program, I arrived to our college classroom to teach my session. Dr. D's session went over by a few minutes, so I sat in back. One of the students, head in her hands, wept at her desk. The night before, in our apartment, I had helped that student prepare her presentation on feminism for Dr. D's class. After class, I asked Dr. D why the student was crying. "What are you talking about?" he said, and kept walking. Over lunch, another student told me Dr. D had degraded the crying student's presentation. "He was way too harsh with her," he said. It was clear that Dr. D was capable of anything, including using a student as a tool to admonish me, a student he knew I had worked with.

In London, he ran off with metro-sexual boys from our class, to bars, to get stoned in his room (the sweet smell wafted under the door). At breakfast, I'd hear stories of drunken escapades from hung over students who could barely hold their forks. "Last night," one student said, "I had to pee so bad when we were out. Dr. D pointed to a tree and told me to pee behind it and I did!" Another student said she'd never gotten drunk before, but added, "I had so much fun but now I feel like barfing."

Given that we were the only authority figures, the "parents" of these students (most were barely twenty-years old), Dr. D was clearly the "fun" parent. I held my tongue. I fumed. A student knocked on my door at 7 a.m. to complain about Dr. D. "He only gives attention to a small group of guys," she said. "A bunch of us feel left out."

I told the student I'd talk to him. When the class went on a tour of a school, we sat on a bench and waited. I told Dr. D about the student complaint, how I also observed him hanging around with a small cohort of male students.

He looked straight ahead, a confused expression. "You know I think you're wonderful, don't you?"

Before we could get far in the conversation, the students showed up.

After arriving back to North Carolina, I told the chair. I told colleagues. Evident Dr. D manipulated most everyone in my department, no one believed me, or believed me enough to do anything about it. In fact, most of my colleagues praised Dr. D's contributions to the department. He won teaching awards. A handful of colleagues, apparently influenced by him, ignored me in the hallway. My only ally, a new hire from out of state, didn't have much sway. Dr. D sat her down and told her not to associate with me. "She's a malevolent force in the department," he said. Like me, she saw through Dr. D's snake-like charm and stayed away from him. When it came time for her three-year review, Dr. D and his minions orchestrated a full-on attack against her reappointment, claiming she only cared about her own writing, despite her glowing student evaluations.

I told everyone I knew—acquaintances, friends, family—about Dr. D, making sure to describe his small red eyes and hyena laugh. With each telling, I relived the pain of not being seen or heard, of paralysis, of letting the situation keep me up at night. During his tenure vote, everyone voted yes. Except me. Before it was official, I met with a high-up administrator to tell her what I knew, to tell her that students were willing to come forward. She said the ball was rolling too fast, tenure for Dr. D was certain.

I continued to complain to anyone who'd listen. For five years.

Now, before the exercise, Kim had told the two participants in the workshop (me and an older chatty Southern woman) about the exercise's goal of establishing clear boundaries by developing an awareness—our own and in relation to the horse—so we could find, as she said, "a place of perfect harmony between the two of you."

Or in Dr. D's case, the only place of harmony would have been to establish clear boundaries to begin with, to not engage on any personal level, to trust my gut. Instead, like I'd done time and time again with romantic interests, I opened up too quickly, making myself vulnerable, ripe for attack.

"What do you do," Kim had asked, "if someone moves into your personal space?"

"You back up," I said.

"Or if you step towards the person," Kim said, "they usually back away."

Precisely why I stepped into Zorro's path.

We tried the exercise again. This time I let my guard down. While Zorro chewed hay at the opposite end of the corral, I ambled towards him. He continued to eat, glimpsing at me with his right eye. About fifteen feet away, I said, "This is the point where I'm comfortable."

"Walk two steps closer," Kim said.

I did, and it didn't feel comfortable.

"Step back," she said. "How does that feel?"

It felt safe. I had established my comfort point.

"What did you learn about yourself?" Kim asked.

"It's easier to step out of the way than be barreled over."

Kim asked the other participant, the chatty woman, to find her place of comfort with Zorro. While he chewed on hay in a corner of the corral, the chatty woman slowly walked towards him. He turned away from her, rattled the water bucket and banged his head against the gate. He clearly wanted out. But the chatty woman kept walking.

Kim asked her to stop. "What did you learn from the exercise?"

"Well," the chatty woman said, making the word into three syllables. "I guess I have a tendency to overstep my boundaries."

"Sometimes we humans," Kim said, "get set in our own agenda and ignore, in this instance, Zorro's clear communication that he didn't want contact. His place of comfort was across the corral."

The chatty woman shook her head and extended her arms as if ready to catch a falling cat. "All I wanted to do," she said, "was pet the horse!"

As long as I continued to get riled up about Dr. D's behaviors, I, rightly so at first, gave those thoughts power. But after Kim's workshop, I started to push thoughts of Dr. D away, knowing I'd done everything I could.

A friend of mine from grad school advised me to keep away from him. "He'll eventually pick on someone else."

I kept away. I didn't talk about him. I said hello to him, and the other colleagues who stared at their shoes while they passed in the hallway. When thoughts of frustration and anger about Dr. D drifted into my mind, I made gratitude lists. Within the year, more students complained about him and his late-night Skype calls to handsome boys (one told me he never saw Dr. D's hands). Another student told me Dr. D had tripped on mushrooms while he drove her ex-boyfriend and another freshman boy to the local hot springs. The new chair, the patriarch of our department, gave Dr. D a talking to, warned him to quit his inappropriate behavior. Now Dr. D claimed the new chair was harassing him and filed a grievance. He made the new chair's life miserable.

Lawyers and parents and private detectives got involved. Within months, Dr. D disappeared. I suspect he was forced to resign. One colleague said, "He told me awful things about you." I didn't want to know any details. It didn't matter. What mattered was my life had become lighter when I opened myself up to gratitude, when I stepped away from darkness. Of course it didn't hurt that karma caught up with Dr. D, that the colleagues who ignored me finally saw through his manipulation, that we all breathed a collective sigh.

After Dr. D's departure, Kim invited me to work with Zorro again. She led me into the corral, where Zorro grazed. This time I felt rested and confident. Once again, Kim asked me to find my place of comfort. I walked towards the horse. His tail swished and he walked away. When I walked in the opposite direction, he trotted towards me. We played a comfortable game of push and pull, of leader and follower, switching roles until he turned and stepped in front of me. Now we faced each other, eye to eye. I reached out and caressed his mane. And burst into tears.

Kim asked, "What did you learn about yourself?"

This is what a healthy relationship should feel like," I said. "A comfortable dance. A place of mutual respect."

"Why do you think you cried?" she asked.

Maybe I cried for letting myself get barreled over, time and time again; maybe I thought that's all I deserved. Or maybe I grieved for all the armor I had piled onto myself, the hardened shell that made it tough for anyone to get through, even when I didn't need it. Or the times I should have used it to protect me from Dr. D and others, whom I blindly opened myself up to at first, when I needed it most. The word *armor* is one letter away from *amor*; maybe I cried for the many times I confused the two. Or maybe those tears acknowledged a cleansing, demonstrated not only by my trust in Zorro, but in myself, to know when danger barrels towards me, I have the strength and wherewithal to shove it away.

DRESS UP *as a* LITERARY FIGURE

1

EVERY STUDENT IN MY QUEER THEORY GRADUATE SEMINAR lusted after our professor—just the right mix of tough yet nurturing, an intellectual powerhouse, a preppy "academic dyke" in starched blazers and khakis. It didn't matter if we identified as straight or gay, male or female, bi or trans. After class we drank pitchers of beer at a local bar and talked about her intense eyes, her fit body, her chiseled features, how she stared at whomever made a comment in class and said, "Tell me more," how she said, "Questions are good, answers are better," how each of us left her office drenched in sweat after meeting with her to discuss our midterm paper. She had no problem indoctrinating us into examining sexuality through a Marxist perspective, connecting capitalism and identity, the working class, queerness, and the pink dollar. I worked my ass off for her.

For my final paper, I analyzed two lesbian films to demonstrate how the plots of both were surprisingly similar. In *Desert Hearts* and *When Night is Falling*, the unhappily married, uptight English professor falls for the sexy "other"—the ranch hand in *Desert Hearts*, and the circus acrobat in *When Night is Falling*. Both professors, literally and metaphorically, let their hair down by the end, and in both films, the conclusions are ambiguous, making the films marketable for all audiences—straight audiences may conclude the professors had their flings and will get on with their "normal" lives, and queer audiences might feel satisfied with an implied queer happily-ever-after ending.

I presented a version of this paper at a conference during my first year of teaching college full-time. A student of mine, let's call her Sally, came up to me after the panel and said, "So Professor, when are *you* going to let your hair down?"

A piece of me felt a tinge of excitement—to be the object of desire by a brilliant student. I kept my distance, but the situation confused me. In fact, I told my then-girlfriend—not to make her jealous, but to reassure her and myself that nothing would ever happen. Maybe I needed to name it, even if it suggested culpability.

Sally often plopped herself down in my office, usually wearing a suggestive tank top. After asking an obligatory question about a class assignment, she asked personal questions about grad school or my younger days in New York. One day she asked why I didn't have a dog.

"I have wanderlust," I said. "Can't make a commitment to take care of a dog."

A week later, in her fictional story, the lesbian narrator asks her girlfriend why she doesn't have a dog. The girlfriend replies, "I have wanderlust. Can't make a commitment."

Again I felt a tiny thrill. Yet the thrill disgusted me. This student was a good fifteen years younger, and on top of that, I was her teacher. Thank heavens she was about to graduate. She even invited me to her graduation party. "A bunch of other professors," she said, "will be there too." A male colleague convinced me to go and offered to accompany me, even though I knew better than to attend. At the party, he had fun watching Sally follow me around, while her boyfriend followed her. Before leaving, she walked my colleague and me down the driveway and said, "Your grades will be in by Monday, right? I'll call you on Tuesday."

She never called but six months later, she grated Parmesan cheese into my lap at an Italian restaurant where she waitressed.

"Oh, sorry," she said, before grating more onto my plate of spaghetti.

I brushed the cheese off my pants, no longer wanting to play this mixed-up game of power and desire.

2

JENNY, ONCE A STUDENT in my creative writing class, came to an English Department Halloween Party dressed as *me*. *Dress up as a literary figure*, the invitation read. One student came as Sylvia Plath, her head in an oven. Another student came as James Joyce, a frame around his head. I suppose, if you want to push the definition, I can be construed as a literary figure.

Great way to pay homage, one could say. Embarrassed, maybe flattered, I felt like a mother/mentor to Jenny. She mentioned that her mother was Jewish, her father a Southern Baptist. "That's a recipe for disaster," she said. Three years before, her mother had succumbed to ovarian cancer. Now she lived with her Baptist grandmother.

The charming, smart, talented fuck-up, Jenny wrote edgy, hilarious tales—one about her grandmother finding a bagful of Jenny's dildos and setting them out on the kitchen table for her to see when she arrived home.

A few hours after she left the Halloween party, she sent me an email: *Hey, I am drunk, and to be honest and I am still dressed like you. I wanted to say you are absolutely beautiful. Fuck, I wish I wasn't drunk. I'm sorry. Good night.*

I ignored the email, wished I never got it.

Another student wrote about a wild crush she had on her high school film teacher, a man in his late sixties with bad teeth and a comb-over—an example of how the thrill of intellectually engaging in new ideas can ignite our physical bodies. I understand how students could easily displace this desire onto a teacher, like I did with my Queer Theory professor. Perhaps the physical desire I had for her was wrapped in an emotional yearning for a nurturing mother—one who could give me the attention and guidance I never received from my own mother.

Jenny dropped out of school and worked full time at a fast-food restaurant. She got pregnant and married the manager. The night before she gave birth, she wrote me an email:

Lori! I'm typing on my phone but simply put, I wanted to say: you know I love you, right? Yeah, I feel completely lame now, but last night, I lay there wondering what I should say to you. So I'm finally saying something. I miss you. I think about you every day, like every day since I've met you. I'd give anything to just sit and talk to you right now. Please let me know you've read this. Most importantly, please don't hate me.

I was mortified. A few weeks later, she apologized and blamed it on crazy hormones. She asked to meet and we met for coffee at Starbucks. I told her she should be grateful for her beautiful child and husband. She said, "I am, but I'm a goddamn lesbian."

She could have been a "goddamn lesbian," but she also could have been searching for a mother/mentor figure to guide her, give her approval, give her a hug, which I did before I drove away.

3

DURING MY THIRD YEAR TEACHING FULL-TIME, I put a conference panel together at school: "Bodies in the Classroom." I asked two colleagues to join me. Although I talked about my intentions before the presentation—how to deal with the fact we're not disembodied, how students will develop crushes, how we're human with emotions and reactions, both colleagues neglected to mention anything about this in their talk. One focused on student evaluations that commented on the professor's physical appearance, how being a female professor has its own challenges; the other spoke about responding to students who made comments about her clothes and hair.

Surely, I wasn't the only one who dealt with student crushes.

I started off by telling the story of receiving anonymous gifts under my door—poems, feathers, and postcards with messages such as *You're a great teacher.* After matching up the anonymous handwriting with an attendance sign-in sheet, I had to figure out how to confront the student. I called the counseling center; I conferred with colleagues. Since the student made an appointment to discuss her writing with me, I brought it up then. "I have reason to believe you're leaving me notes and gifts," I said.

"What do you mean?" she said. "How do you know it's me?"

"Your handwriting," I said.

"You've never seen my handwriting!"

With evidence, she backed down.

"We need to have clear boundaries," I said, "between teacher and student." I also told her it makes me uncomfortable to get anonymous notes, even with the best intentions.

"I didn't realize it made you uncomfortable," she said. "Sorry."

In private, two colleagues thanked me for my courage to bring up the topic, as if broaching it in public was an admission of guilt.

4

I CALLED A STUDENT OUT FOR TEXTING IN CLASS; she snapped back, acted as if she had every right to do whatever the hell she pleased. Although I don't have children, I assume this is what it feels like to have a rebellious child and lose control. Now that I've been teaching for over two decades, and I'm at least the age of my students' mothers (or grandmothers), I suspect my "teacher crush" status has run its course, and if anything, I'm firmly in the mother category, especially when it comes to defiant students. That's how it felt when Frankie, a whip-smart undergraduate with spiky pink hair, raised her hand at the beginning of my Queer Theory class. I had asked for general comments about a novel I assigned. "I'm disappointed in you," she said, "as a mentor and professor, that you didn't give us a trigger warning. The sexual violence in the novel could have re-traumatized someone."

The class fell silent. "Thank you for letting me know," I said. "I'll do that if I teach this book in the future." I moved on but wrote her an email and said she should have talked to me before class instead of publicly airing her disgruntlement. She later read my department chair the short sexual assault scene. She told him she didn't feel safe in my class. He asked her why she didn't put the book down.

I wrote Frankie another email and asked if she'd speak with me; I wanted her to feel safe. I wanted to feel safe, too. In my office, she wept and apologized. She told me about her mother who kicked her out of the house after finding out she was queer. She told me she had to work two jobs to pay for school. She told me she didn't put the book down because she had OCD and needed to finish what she started. She told me this was her third attempt at finishing college. She told me she wrote short stories and wanted me to read her work. She told me she wanted to keep in touch when the semester ended. She asked, at the end of our meeting, if we could hug, and we hugged.

§

THE LAST TIME I ATTENDED A NEW AGE SPIRITUAL CHURCH, I ran into a former student, Carla. In class, she interrupted and told long-winded stories in a loud, husky voice. She had a frail frame and blonde bob. She also coughed and wheezed. When she opened her mouth, other students' eyes rolled. In class she mentioned she had cystic fibrosis. The average life span for people who live to adulthood with the disease is thirty-seven years; I tried to be patient and show compassion. But one day my patience ran out. I asked her to stay after class so we could talk.

"I love how enthusiastic you are," I said.

Carla looked out the window, jiggled her leg.

"And your response papers are excellent," I said, "but part of participation is listening, letting others have the opportunity to share."

Now both legs jiggled. "My mother says the same thing!" she yelled. "You don't care about me! You could give a shit about me!" Her body sprung up. She ran away.

Later she apologized and tried to limit her talking but, as if unscrewing the top of a shaken-up carbonated drink, she jabbered on until the fizz ran out. Towards the end of the semester, she told me how much she had learned in class, how she never considered herself a feminist until now and thanked me for opening doors that might have remained shut.

"Thank you for telling me," I said. "It means a lot." When she left my office, my shoulders relaxed.

For a final project, she made a 'zine that was a feminist critique of women comic strip characters. An hour before the last class, a librarian called: "One of your students was hyperventilating," she said. "I brought her to the counseling center." Carla had spent hours trying the get the photocopying of the 'zine just right.

Now at church, Carla and I made eye contact. Her jaw twisted. She took a deep breath. Her body shuddered. She exhaled and called my name. She introduced me to her boyfriend.

During the interlude, we hugged. I held her delicate frame. We wished each other peace.

Six months later, Carla died, not from cystic fibrosis, but in a car crash.

When I learned of her death, I cried and replayed our last interaction at church. On my way out, I had told her how glad I was to run into her.

"Goodbye Professor," she said, beaming, as if a peace offering, making amends with the past. We hugged again, perhaps to make sure we got it right.

And we did.

THE LAST FREIGHT TRAIN

ON FACETIME, MY NEW LOVE INTEREST, Patty, points her phone to show me a freight train chugging by, only a chain-link fence between her backyard and the tracks. I ask how often the train goes by. Maybe two or three times a day, she says. She's not sure. It's ten in the morning and Patty's drinking coffee in her yard. Her face is puffy and tired, and I suspect she had a few too many drinks last night. Maybe that's why she didn't text to let me know she made it home safe. Her battery died, she tells me, and she fell asleep in front of the TV while her phone charged.

I called Patty last night after seeing my friend in the hospital, my friend who'd been in a terrible car accident. "Not sure she's going to make it," I had told Patty.

"So sorry," she said. On her way to a bar to meet friends, Patty assured me she'd text when she got home. She knew I'd worry if I didn't hear from her, that my mind tended to drift to worst-case scenarios.

"Anytime," I said. "I turn my ringer off."

But when I checked my phone at three in the morning and didn't see a message, my gut said it was over—either Patty's life or our relationship.

Patty lived by the Great Smoky Mountains, two hours west of Asheville. After meeting on a dating website, we texted back and forth and learned we had an acquaintance in common. She said she loved my city and sent pictures of her children and went on about her awful ex; I liked that she felt open enough to share personal matters. She said I looked familiar, that maybe we knew each other when we both lived in Manhattan over twenty years before. We made a date to speak on the phone, and when we did, she talked and talked, a little too much. She asked if I wanted to FaceTime. When her face appeared, we both smiled. All the talking didn't matter. We continued to smile. I asked, "When're you coming to Asheville?"

She tapped her lips with her index finger. "Have you seen the Chihuly lights," she said, "at the Biltmore?"

Two weeks later, she sat across from me at a restaurant. She looked tired, but it was late and her drive took an hour longer than it should have. We chatted about her ex, her kids, our jobs. I kept looking at her, the way she lifted her beer mug, the way she lowered her eyes when talking about her ex. Was I even attracted to her? Before she left to find her hotel, we briefly hugged. My first thought: nice enough but not interested. She texted to let me know her room was cozy. I texted back: "It was great to finally meet you."

"Back at you," she said.

"And what did you think?" I asked.

"About what?"

"About me," I said.

"You're just as smart," she said, "and cute in person. And what about me?"

"You're really sweet. I sense there's a sadness lurking inside of you."

"You're very intuitive," she said.

The next day, we took a walk. I still didn't feel anything more than a friendship. We went out for dinner with her pal who had just moved to the area. I took note of the four drinks Patty had, maybe more—the beer, the wine, the mixed drink. Then again, I had a beer and a vodka drink.

Something in me shifted. Maybe it was her hearty laugh, or the way she listened to her friend and nodded, a much younger friend. She considered herself a mentor of sorts to this friend, and maybe it was the way her friend brought out Patty's maternal side. Or maybe the alcohol loosened her up. After dinner, she asked if I wanted to go to a bar. I said I was tired but I'd see her in the morning. We hugged. It was more than a friend hug.

On her last night in town, we kissed. She spent the night in my guest room.

In the morning we held hands and strolled in the woods. I told her about my long string of alcoholic exes. Patty said, "I don't even know what an alcoholic is. What's an alcoholic?"

I stopped in my tracks and looked at her. "Please don't say that!" I said. "The last person who said that, a woman I had dated a while back, turned out to be a complete alcoholic."

"I don't drink alone," Patty said. "And I don't like to have drunken sex."

I didn't tell her that the same ex said exactly those words.

Yet maybe Patty was different. After all, she was a doctor. She worked hard. She had three kids. She had to be responsible.

And she was a good kisser.

When we talked on the phone, she never mentioned booze. "Connection is important," I told Patty. "We don't have to talk or text all the time, but a few texts a day would be great." She said she understood. (I didn't tell her how anxious I'd get if I didn't hear back after several hours, how my abandonment issues would kick in. But I did tell her I was working on my anxiety issues with a therapist.)

Patty introduced me to her children on FaceTime. She wanted to visit again, to take me out for an early birthday dinner, wherever I wanted to go.

The day before Patty's arrival, I ran into a friend who knew of Patty. She said I needed to be careful. She wouldn't give details. "She's good looking," my friend said.

I wouldn't let up; I needed to know.

"You didn't hear this from me," my friend said. "I heard Patty's a big drinker."

My heart sank. I couldn't sleep. But I told myself the friend who revealed the information never even met Patty. Maybe Patty's heavy drinking days were over. Or maybe I just needed to confirm what my gut already knew.

The second time she visited, she drank two beers. But we only spent one night together. I asked Patty if we had anything in common. "We both like nature," she said, "and we both like dogs." Maybe that was enough.

Maybe anxiety is part of my DNA. After all, I'm a New York Jew, and a Virgo. In psychological terms, I'm a poster child for the ambivalent-anxious attachment personality, according to attachment theory, which originates with the work of psychologist John Bowlby. In the 1930s, Bowlby considered the importance of a child's relationship with their mother. At times, the mother's response to a child who exhibits ambivalent-anxious attachment personality is nurturing, but at other times it's insensitive. The child is confused and insecure, not knowing what to expect. They often feel distrustful of their parents, but at the same time act clingy and desperate. As adults, they seek reassurance from others. Deep-seated feelings of rejection make them not trusting of and overly dependent on their partner. In the 1970s, psychologist Mary Ainsworth expanded upon Bowlby's theories. She described three major styles of attachment (similar to Bowlby's)—ambivalent-insecure (I'll refer to this as anxious), secure (the caregiver is sensitive to the child's needs and responds appropriately), and avoidant-insecure (I'll refer to this as avoidant). The parents of avoidant children discourage crying, encourage independence, and have little or no response when the child is distressed. These children avoid conflict by distancing themselves. As adults, avoidant personalities manifest in the form of addicts, workaholics, or any activity that helps dull out painful emotions.

Unconsciously, according to attachment theory, the anxious and avoidant personalities seek each other out. Reenacting childhood dynamics, these relationships are familiar and exciting, yet make us anxious types even more anxious.

I can't say for sure how my past romantic partners were raised—I know that other factors come into play when it comes to addictions, but when I look at my own behavior, attachment theory neatly aligns with how my mother raised me. I begged for attention. My brother said I'd wear her down, and she'd finally listen to me, look at me.

Patty and I spent a third weekend together. She came to a literary reading I organized. She sat at the bar and bought my friends pints while I hosted the event. Later, I recoiled from the smell of her beer breath. She insisted she wasn't drunk. I told myself not to judge her. We danced in my living room. We held each other tight.

She texted sweet messages with kissy face emoticons. We talked about meeting up in Paris, in New York. Her Chihuahua sat in her lap during our FaceTime conversations. Once I heard the freight train chug by.

In my twenties, my first long-term boyfriend smoked pot daily and charmed me with his humor. But his mood changed like a lightning snap—when I beat him in a game of chess, when I wouldn't lend him money to buy pot. These rages felt familiar. This was passion. This was love.

My next long-term relationship was with a woman. She was kind. Sweet. Smart. Funny. Yet I never felt the same passion. Besides, I wasn't ready to come out. But I loved her. We laughed together, created art together. In retrospect, I likely didn't feel the passion because she had a secure attachment personality. I didn't know how to receive her kindness, her nurturing. I felt confused, frustrated, guilty. Besides, anxious types like myself aren't attracted to secure personalities. We need the avoidant personality to fuel the passion.

After the freight train chugged by her yard, Patty told me she needed to find new friends who weren't heavy drinkers. She said she needed to stay home to take care of her daughter, who was sick with an awful cold.

"Who are your close friends?" I asked. "Who do you call when you have a problem?"

"I don't talk about my problems with friends," she said.

Patty had drinking buddies. When she's drinking, she said, nothing else matters.

Later that afternoon, on Facebook, Patty wrote *Drinking beer with friends*, accompanied by a picture of her hoisting a mug.

The next morning, she didn't feel well. She said she needed to stay in. But she later went out dancing, said she'd text when she got home. She didn't text.

I said I was done. She cried, said she'd work on things. She said she had given up on herself. The only reason she was alive was because of her children. "Please don't go away from me," she said.

"If I visit," I asked, "could we have a sober weekend?"

"If we go to dinner, I'll have a beer," she said.

My gut hurt.

My friend I had visited in the hospital was moved to a hospice care facility.

Avoiders don't want anyone putting restrictions on their freedoms. They don't worry about relationships ending. If a relationship is threatened, they bury their feelings of distress.

Patty wanted her freedom. And so did I.

Estimates vary, but some psychologists say that half the population has a secure attachment personality. In general, secure people find other secure people and stay in long-term relationships. The remaining personality types make up the other half—avoidant (30%) and anxious (20%). Thus, if we take away the secure personalities from the dating pool, a majority of those left are avoidant. Enough for me to continue to find another aphrodisiac, to hop on the avoidant freight train packed with highly flammable explosives.

Just like Patty sought escape from painful emotions through booze, she provided me with the familiar excitement of yet another unmanageable relationship with the avoidant personality, the partner who validates my abandonment fears and beliefs about not being loveable, not being enough.

But I was enough for Patty, at least when we walked through the Chihuly exhibit at the Biltmore Estate. We found an empty deck overlooking the Blue Ridge Mountains. I touched her shoulder and she wrapped her arm around my waist and I nuzzled her neck, and it felt like a first kiss was on its way. But a group of Japanese tourists descended upon us, so we continued to walk through the exhibit. That night, in my living room, I booted my dog off the futon, again and again, and we finally kissed—a luscious and forever and so full of hope kiss.

"I could swear," Patty said, "I've met you before. Or at least seen you before."

"I lived on the Lower East Side of Manhattan," I said.

Patty leaned her head on her elbow and stared at me. "I used to go to poetry readings on the Lower East Side."

"Maybe you saw me," I said, "read poetry at one of those readings."

Patty nodded. "Maybe I did." She pulled me toward her. "Come here my poet girl."

A friend I hadn't seen in a while asked if I was dating anyone.

"I just broke up," I said, "with yet another blonde drinker. At least she was a sweet drunk."

He laughed and shook his head. "When will you break the cycle?"

"I hope I'm done," I said. "I'm tired."

And there *is* hope. Research shows a person's attachment style could change—a partner who acts as a reliable security figure can restore a sense of safety and help the anxious person function more securely.

My friend, who never regained consciousness after her accident, died in hospice.

Two days after I last talked to Patty, I dreamt a freight train chugged by an abandoned factory. Suddenly, one of the train cars bolted up and exploded on the other side of the tracks, leaving behind only rubble and smoke.

In the dream I was safe. I could walk away. After the smoke cleared, I did just that.

MY HISTORY *of* WAITING

I TELL MY NEW THERAPIST ABOUT the moment I learned of my mother losing her life in a car accident, how ever since that day I've had trouble sleeping. She asks me to stay in that thought while a small vibrating device pulses back and forth from my right hand to left hand and back. This bilateral stimulation is supposed to help mitigate the effects of trauma. But I'm distracted by the loud ticks of a wall clock. I'm trying to ignore the ticks but the more I try, the louder they get.

As a four and five year old, I cried when my mother left for work. I asked over and over, "Are you really leaving?" When the car pulled from the driveway I sobbed. If she didn't return by four o' clock, I stared out my bedroom window and waited. By 4:15, if she still hadn't returned, I imagined the worst. Twenty years later, she died in the passenger seat of a Nissan Sentra.

For my eighth birthday, my mother gave me a ladybug alarm clock. I didn't notice the loud ticks for a good month, until the ticks echoed in my head, becoming louder and louder, as if they tapped a little hammer against my brain. I wrapped the clock in towels and stuffed it in my closet and never used it again.

The therapist asks me to stay with the thought of the young girl looking out for her mother, and the vibrating device again pulses from hand to hand. I think of my history of waiting. Of longing. Longing to see a girlfriend who lives across the country. Waiting for the phone to ring. I think of other romantic partners—the German I met in Spain who ignored me for hours and wouldn't tell me why, and when she finally did, she said it bothered her that I didn't know how to hold my fork the European way. Or the English woman who brought along a guy friend, who was more than a friend, on our getaway to Rumania, or the Spaniard who stared out the train window and wouldn't talk to me after I told her the train's exhaust made me nauseous. Now, when the vibrations stop, the ticking of the clock takes over, but I don't say anything. I don't want to come off as too crazy or sensitive.

Again, I'm asked to contemplate my last thought, and the device pulses and I think of my romantic involvement with partners at a distance. I lost my virginity to a man I met while on vacation in California—3000 miles from my home, and the first women I kissed lived in England—how I've been more open to romantic partners at a distance, whether physically or emotionally, or both. More open to those I had to long for, keeping my heart sealed off, protected.

To long for is from the Old English: "to yearn after, to grieve for," literally, "to grow long, lengthen." As a noun, a longing is "a strong, persistent desire or craving, especially for something unattainable or distant."

Like my mother—unattainable and distant. Lost in a world of shopping, hoarding and television. I longed for her attention, her love. I begged and screamed for it. "Listen to me!" I said, over and over. "Stop screaming," she said. When I left for college, I gave up. And began my journey for the unattainable mate. If available, I had no interest, felt no spark, no passion. Or maybe fear kept me at arm's length—fear of abandonment, of losing at love.

Instead I gave myself no chance of winning; instead I opened my heart to highly combustible partners (and they towards me); inevitably, the union smoldered until a lone smoke plume hissed and fizzled.

Only after he transferred to a college three hours north did I get involved with my first serious boyfriend. Three years before, a month into my freshman year, he wanted to date me, but I said, "I'm flattered. We're friends." So my roommate dated him. She kicked me out of our room to be with him. Maybe it was safer to long for him from the other side of the door.

The therapist asks how I'm doing, if I need to take a break. I tell her I'm doing okay but still don't tell her about the distracting clock. Or how I'm not sure she knows what she's doing. Again she turns on the vibrating device and asks me to stay in my last thought. But I could only think of the clock. The ticks. The tocks. How time keeps moving, how even if I wrapped up the ladybug alarm clock, it didn't stop time, it only muffled it, how twenty years have gone by since I moved from Manhattan to Asheville for my professor job, how I was a fresh-faced thirty-something and where did that time go? Now I'm a not-so fresh-faced fifty-something who is more aware of that ticking clock—not just the ticks but what the ticks mean—I don't have much time left; those twenty years whizzed by without warning. At a conference I recently attended, a thirty-something woman I befriended referred to me as a "cool older woman." How did I become "a cool *older* woman?"

Pulitzer-Prize winning poet Mary Oliver recently died at the age of 83. Over a decade ago, I had volunteered to pick her up from a hotel and bring her to my school to give a reading. Warned that she chain-smoked, I kept my car windows open. My friend rode in the back seat. She said Oliver flicked a cigarette butt out the window. Maybe Oliver had good genes to live so long as a chain smoker. Or maybe creative pursuits counteracted the effects of smoking. Creative pursuits, scientists say, add years to one's life. I think about a line from an Oliver poem: "Instructions for living a life. Pay Attention. Be astonished. Tell about it."

I'm paying attention. And telling you I've always made time to create: music, art, writing. Maybe that's what counteracted my addiction—longing for the unavailable—the alcoholics, the cutters, the shopaholics, those who lived across the country or on another continent. When it didn't work out, I could blame it on the distance, the alcohol. Never take the blame myself—the person who embarked on these romances doomed from the start, pining for a partner who might be there, but not there. Like longing for my mother. There, in her bedroom, watching television. There, in the kitchen, on the telephone.

The therapist asks me to close my eyes. She asks about my last thought. I say, "Emptiness. Frustration." She says, "Start with that thought." And the clock ticks get louder and the vibrating pulse moves from hand to hand and I think about how maybe I never really opened my heart fully, how I couldn't, while time kept on ticking and the worry-line on my forehead deepened.

In those twenty years since moving to Asheville, a number of my colleagues have retired or died. Now I'm one of the elders on the hall. Another colleague is dying after battling cancer for five years. I visit her and we talk about death, the meaning of life. She accepts that her life will be cut short but tells me she's happy. She asks if I'm still dating the woman I had last told her about. I shake my head. "Another blonde alcoholic," I say. "I'm done. Really."

In the past she has said, "Hope springs eternal"—a phrase from Alexander Pope's "Essay on Man":

> Hope springs eternal in the human breast;
> Man never Is, but always To be blest.
> The soul, uneasy, and confin'd from home,
> Rests and expatiates in a life to come."

My friend doesn't say it now. I don't say I'm sick of waiting for "a life to come."

This longing business is exhausting. I've had adventures in faraway lands but always came home alone, my heart intact, protected. Like my grandma Becky's couch wrapped in plastic. No chance of stains or rips; yet no chance to relish in its softness.

And so I continue the trauma of losing my mother, of feeling like I never had a mother, of searching far and wide for a love that can't return the favor. Grandma Becky spent her last year in a hospital bed. She always asked what day it was, what time it was. I never understood why she would care. But now I do. It was a way to feel control in a world where she had none.

The therapist again asks about my thought. I finally tell her about the clock. I can't focus. The ticks are deafening. I've always been sensitive to noise, especially repetitive noises. She asks if she should put the clock in the hallway. I say yes. "You're not the only one," she says, "who has a problem with the clock." She puts it on the other side of the door. I tell her how I never thought about time, how I don't have much of it left.

I don't tell her how distance and longing have kept me from getting what I craved, that I've known my mother dead longer than I've known her alive, that no matter how much I screamed and cried she couldn't soothe me, that she probably didn't have the wherewithal to soothe herself, that the best thing I could do is peel away my heart's protective coating, to feel its softness, to let it breathe, to let the trapped yet familiar grief disperse so I could sleep. I don't tell her that these pulsing devices in my hands might as well be my beating heart, that there are only so many beats left, that I need to use them wisely.

LESBIAN CINDERELLA

1

I HAD A SHORT-LIVED ROMANCE with a long-distance woman who drank one Bloody Mary after the next. She visited for five days and spent most of that time in bed while she fought an awful cold. I asked if she wanted an old pair of my Doc Martens. She raised her leg and I slid the shoe on. A perfect fit.

"It's like the lesbian Cinderella," she said.

The same shoes that left blisters on my feet.

"Dating is a dance," my therapist said. "Sometimes you lead, sometimes you follow, as long as there's a balance." But when dating a heavy drinker, there is no leading and following, only stumbling. Stumbling home, stumbling to bed, stumbling away.

2

A WOMAN I MET ON MATCH.COM asked what my deal-breakers were.

"Heavy drinkers, smokers, loud chewers and people who crack gum," I said.

She didn't understand. "Chewing a piece of gum is a deal-breaker?"

I asked if she wanted to Skype since she lived across the state. She suggested we talk on the phone. She said her (one blurry) picture should be enough to see what she looked like. She told me about a woman she went on a date with. "She asked me to take my boots off," she said, "before I entered her apartment. I thought that was rude."

"Some people are sensitive to street dirt," I said, "and don't want it tracked in their home."

"I like heel power," she said.

I didn't say it but thought *what the hell is heel power*? I get that there's a time and place for a woman to feel strong and empowered in choosing her own shoes, but in this instance, "heel power" felt like grasping for control—not only over her feet, but also over her image—her blurred image, the only indication of what she might have looked like, probably taken years before.

3

ON SEVERAL OCCASIONS, an ex-girlfriend insisted on buying me shoes, even when I wasn't with her. "I just sent you a pair of Sketchers. They're like slipping your feet into velvet."

"My feet are messed up," I told her. "Most shoes don't fit me."

"You're so unappreciative," she said. "At least you could try them on."

Of course I tried them on, just like I tried her on. And if she were a shoe, sharp pebbles would have dug into the soles of my feet. I walked in those metaphorical shoes for nine months, thinking the pebbles would disappear, or maybe I'd adapt. But they grew larger and more painful, until I almost stumbled flat on my face, drunk on her words: *You'll never feel alone again*, grasping to those shoes as if they were a life-raft.

4

THANK HEAVENS SHERRY, a woman I dated in grad school, wore red Converse All Stars. She could easily drink a six-pack in one sitting, and drank even more after her parents learned she was romantically involved with a woman. "You're in the grips of Satan," they told her. Full of compassion for everyone but herself, she stumbled around in bars late at night, telling strangers she loved them. Together we played with words, wrote poetry, sang Ani di

Franco songs. "If she doesn't stop drinking," I told her therapist," Sherry by my side, "she'll be dead within the year!" Always sick with worry, I wrote eulogies about her in my head. Yet I couldn't control her drinking. I could only control what shoes I bought before visiting her (leather flats that had a wide toe-box), when I told her I needed to let go, that I'd always be there for her, that I'd always love her. And I have. And I do.

5

THE DAY AFTER CALLING IT QUITS with yet another heavy drinker, I put on a worn pair of hiking boots, its leather molded to my feet, and drove the Blue Ridge Parkway. Surrounded by thick foliage, I sauntered up a trail, stepping over rocks and roots with ease, until I reached a peak, where the view opened up to a panorama of blue ridge pinnacles and sky. I inhaled the majestic view and shook off the lingering remnants of a relationship that included phone calls ending in abrupt hang-ups, always leaving me holding a silent line. By the end, I didn't call back. I didn't try to make peace.

I followed another trail around the mountain, through a stream, in my waterproof boots, my second skin. They supported my ankles and helped me climb steep inclines without tripping over myself. At another pinnacle, crows cawed, and billowy clouds drifted above the pine trees carpeting the mountainside. A giant weight lifted, as if I could walk on water, as if I could fly.

Later that day, I said to a friend, "I'm so done with fucked-up relationships."

"But what will you write about?' she asked. "Isn't that how you get your material?"

"There's plenty to write about. Nature. Dogs. Shoes," I said.

THE END *of* AIR HUGS

LESLIE'S HOSPICE BED LAY SMACK IN THE MIDDLE of a sunny room (just down the hall from where my friend, who was in a terrible car accident, passed away), her gaunt face and bony not-yet-thirty-five year-old body propped up on it, a body withered from a year's worth of surgeries and chemotherapy. She swiped her finger across an iPad. "Just paying some bills," she said, as if paying the mortgage is commonplace in a palliative-care facility.

I settled into a metal chair by her bed.

"How's that woman you were seeing," Leslie asked, "the one from Tennessee?"

"It was fun while it lasted," I said. "But the distance was too much."

Her father and sister sat nearby, talking softly.

In the past, Leslie and I had perused the personal ads together. She took it upon herself to find me a partner. Once she had pointed to a photo of an older white-haired woman stepping out of a Mercedes Benz. "How about her? She looks nice."

"She might be nice, but come on!" I said. "She looks like my grandmother!"

Leslie laughed and said, "All right. Let's keep looking."

Now she paid bills, meeting her obligations before leaving her body and the world.

With a look of concern, Leslie asked, "Any women on the horizon?"

I didn't want to talk about dating prospects to a woman on her deathbed. "Do you want anything," I asked, "from the grocery store?"

"Chocolate," she said. "You know, those bags of little Hershey Bars and Kit Kats."

On the way out, I ran into her partner. "Is it okay if Leslie eats chocolate?"

"She can eat whatever the hell she wants," she said, her curly hair in a frenzy, eyeglasses lopsided on her nose.

"How are you holding up?" I asked.

She sighed, tapped her forehead. "Leslie's in denial. She doesn't want to talk about dying."

I didn't want to talk about it either. How could Leslie, my upbeat friend who carried a bible in her backpack, be dying? While it wasn't rational, I still thought about death in the realm of the old and decrepit.

Fifteen years before, I met Leslie at a literary reading where I shared one of my lesbian dating misadventures. She had just begun to date a friend of mine. "Got any more stories?" she asked. "I'd love to read them!" I sent her a stream of tales. Often she'd write back, "You're so funny! Send more!"

We both attended the local non-denominational church, where during the interlude, we greeted and hugged strangers and wished them peace. I had a hard time hugging friends, let alone strangers. I'd open my arms out wide and pretend to pat a back but not actually touch. As if playing air guitar, I never actually created music. Only pretend music. My friends said I gave a good "air hug." At times, especially with people I didn't know well, hugging felt invasive, like groping without permission. Other times I'd slink away from gatherings without saying goodbye, figuring I'd see my friends again.

Leslie had no problem hugging friends, strangers, homeless clients at the shelter where she volunteered.

I returned to the hospice room with a bag of chocolate, ripped it open and offered it to Leslie. Her yellowed hand picked out two chocolate bars. I asked if she had seen Dede, a mutual friend.

"Nah, haven't seen her in a while," she said, unwrapping a miniature Kit Kat.

Dede later told me she couldn't visit; Leslie's impending death was too upsetting.

Seeing a young, vibrant friend wither into a husk of herself is distressing, but isn't that the least Dede could have done? To say goodbye?

I never had the chance to say goodbye to my mother. It was easier to shut down than beg for affection. Perhaps on an unconscious level, I figured we both had plenty of time to make amends. What would I have done if I had time to say goodbye, if my mother was in the hospice bed? Maybe I'd write a song and sing it for her. Maybe I'd lie next to her and hold her hand, ask her to tell me about her childhood, about what it was like in art school, about regrets she had. Maybe I'd hug her and not let go.

Yet I think of my mother watching television in my childhood home, a glowing blue light reflecting off her bedroom walls. I begged for her attention. In fourth grade, I asked her to listen to me play the clarinet. Too caught up in a television show, she said I needed to wait for the commercials. And during those three minutes, I played "Swing Low, Swing Chariot," yet she continued to gaze at the television. I'd tromp back to my bedroom and watch lots of television, too.

Recently my father, a shriveled man with a full head of hair, asked me to get him a glass of Coke. "You drink soda?" I said. He never drank soda.

Enveloped in his big brown Lazy Boy, he said, "Just half of a glass. What the hell." My father's hands shook. He could no longer walk. Like Leslie eating miniature Hershey bars, shouldn't we find little pleasures where we can? To not hold back and wait?

Leslie exuded a passion for life in the way she hugged, in the way she lived—as if she knew she didn't have much time. At Leslie's memorial service, the minister told the packed church about Leslie's heart, so full of joy, strength and compassion. "When her organs started to shut down," the minister said, "her heart was the last to go."

Once the doctors knew Leslie had a few days of life left in her, she chose to die at home. On Christmas Day, a tree full of tinsel and blinking lights counteracted the somber situation. Leslie sat up in a hospital bed, a big toothy smile on her skeletal face, while friends and family milled about. Her son ran around with his new toy truck. Before I left, Leslie asked, "Any dating prospects on the horizon?"

"I have the worst luck!" I said.

"Keep at it," she said. "It'll happen yet."

Before I left, I hugged Leslie with the same vigor she hugged me with, knowing it would be the last hug we'd exchange. "Merry Christmas," I said.

It took a few more attempts at dating women at a distance, until I understood the need to close the gap, in the way I embraced others, in the way I embraced myself. And it happened. I met a local woman, an available woman. Over the course of the next month and a half, we walked our dogs, attended a dance performance, a gallery opening, and literary readings. At the end of each meeting (we both didn't know if they were "dates"), my hugs became warmer, snugger, until I couldn't let go, until we kissed, and ever since, we've been holding onto each other, just as Leslie predicted.

SEARCH *and* RESCUE

Four months after I lost my long-time companion, Belly, I started to internet puppy date. In the meantime, I left my dog-door open. Maybe Belly's spirit wandered in and out at all hours, like she did when she was alive.

I searched for Border collies or Border collie mixes on shelter websites, Adoptapet, Craigslist, Petfinders, rescue organizations and at local shelters. I loved the smarts, the energy, the regal looks of the Border collie. Maybe I related to the obsessive focus of the Border collie. Maybe it was snobbery. Like the way I searched online for women who earned at least a master's degree.

First up was a Border collie mix puppy advertised on Craigslist. I asked for a photo and what breed she might be mixed with. They thought beagle. But from the picture, the pup looked more like a St. Bernard. I sent the photo to a recent ex—a veterinarian. "All you need," she said, "is a barrel under her neck." I didn't want a big dog. After all, my dog door is medium-sized.

Not sure if the owner intentionally evaded the truth, but in the internet dating arena, I had met plenty of liars, including a woman who said she lived in a big city but actually lived four hours north in a frigid tundra; the same woman who said she didn't know what an alcoholic was but made a point of letting me know she only blacked out once a month. As if that wasn't enough to stop me in my tracks, I traveled up to the tundra and stayed for eight days. Until she blacked out, until I walked the icy streets alone, until my face and feet and heart went numb.

I continued my search for a rescue puppy but came up empty-handed. So I searched breeder websites. A shoe-sized, crazy-eyed Border collie/Aussie popped up. The only pup left from a big litter. Over the phone, the breeder said, "This one here's the smartest, but 'em buyers only care about their markings." I asked a friend to come along—I'd need an extra set of hands if I got the dog. We pulled into the driveway of the breeder's mobile home. In front of us were at least ten pens of Border collies and Australian shepherds, each with at least eight dogs, all woofing and jumping, the stench of shit permeating the place. A frazzled-haired woman held the squirming puppy. She put it on the grass and the dog ran in circles. I leaned down to greet the pup. My friend leaned down and whispered, "Is this a puppy mill?"

The breeder set up a small wired-mesh pen and put the dog in, but the pup crawled up and over the mesh, as if she were a monkey. Breeder woman pointed to a large Border collie tied to a tree: "That's her momma," she said. At first Momma sat still and stared at me, so I walked towards her. Just before I got too close, she bared her teeth and lunged, reminding me of a woman I had met, who looked good on paper—a successful businesswoman who owned a lake-house and invited me for a long weekend. All went well until the third day, when she had one too many drinks and stared out the window and wouldn't talk and it was dark out and I asked what was wrong. As if possessed by the devil, she raged: "I don't know what's worse, if you write about me or don't write about me!" She continued to rage on and off for the rest of the evening. Too paralyzed to leave, I stared at a revolving ceiling fan. In the morning, she apologized, promised it wouldn't happen again. It did.

Next up was a stunning blue merle, a blue-eyed, whitish Border collie pup named Aspen. The breeder lived an hour away and wanted to meet me off I-40, since she'd have to pass through my town on her way across the state. "And by the way," she said, "Aspen's been sold." But Aspen's sister was still available. In the photo, her sister's eyes looked glazed over, as if she might have had a brain injury. When I talked to a geneticist friend, he said, "Do *not* get a blue merle. They're inbred. They have terrible problems—deafness, blindness, who knows what else."

I met a beautiful woman, a Demi Moore double, who lived across the country, who spoke in a language reminiscent of a Harlequin romance novel. I invited her to visit, to be my date at a wedding. She kept up the ruse for twenty-four hours after she landed, until her facial expression turned blank. "What's going on?" I asked.

"I have a girlfriend," she said.

"So why'd you visit?"

"We deserved a beautiful weekend together, and we got it."

A volunteer from the local animal shelter texted: "A sweet one-year old Border collie mix just came in. Get here as soon as you can!" The dog, probably mixed with an English springer spaniel, had been seized from a hoarding situation. A shelter worker snapped a leash on her and handed it to me. "She's never been on a leash before," he said. The dog froze up and, as if the barks of the other dogs were grenades, she tucked her head and tail in. Finally I cajoled the dog to the street. She looked around as if just regaining her vision after years of blindness. Perhaps I wasn't the right person—she had a lot of baggage, more than I could handle. Then again, that never stopped me when it came to internet dating, like when I met R, who lived in New Mexico. Her mother physically abused her. Her ex-girlfriend degraded her, broke up with her, then flaunted a new girlfriend in front her. As soon as I came into the picture, the ex-girlfriend proclaimed her renewed love for R. I didn't wait around to see if R went back, but I suspect she did.

On Petfinders.com, a Border-collie/Jack Russell puppy, Sadie, appeared—a squat black and white wind-up toy of a dog. I drove two hours to meet her. She hid between her foster mother's legs and wouldn't make eye contact. When I tried to pick her up, she howled and ran in circles and barked at neighbors, reminding me of a woman I met on Tinder, who lived with her mother. Over dinner, she told me her last girlfriend would come for the weekend, but by the second day, her mother would whisper, "When is she leaving?" And the woman would say, "I don't know! I hope soon!"

Back online, I found a beautiful Border collie pup in Tennessee. The breeder sent more photos and I said yes. Something about her eyes reminded me of Belly. Intelligent and sensitive. Actually, she looked just like a baby Belly. She'd never be Belly, but yes, I'd pay $1000. Maybe name her Juniper. The breeder wanted to meet me off I-40, said her husband was working on the house and it was too dangerous to come there. Now suspicious that she didn't want me to see a puppy mill like the one I had seen, I said, "But I want to meet her parents." "I'll bring her mother with me," she said. I didn't feel comfortable meeting her off the highway and asked if there was any way I could meet at her house; I didn't have to go in. Finally she gave me her address. I Googled it. Her home was seven hundred square feet on a tenth of an acre and cost $18,000 in 2003. No way she could care for all those dogs advertised on her website, which featured Border collies frolicking on rolling green hills. Nonetheless, I agreed to get the dog. The day before the exchange, I received an email: "Bad news. I brought the dogs in to be assessed for activity level and the dog you wanted was assessed at super high level. She needs a lot of mental and physical stimulation. She can't get that in a regular home. But I'd be glad to sell you her brother, assessed at a retriever level." I didn't want her brother. Perhaps she found someone who'd seal the deal at a highway rest stop.

Maybe I wasn't supposed to get a purebred Border collie. Besides, I shouldn't support breeders, especially breeders who want to meet off of Interstate-40. And, as a friend said, "As long as dogs are dying in shelters, there is no such thing as a responsible breeder." Once again I searched through rescue websites. A new puppy appeared on Adoptapet—a Border collie/shepherd mix. Her name: Panda. A tiny panda bear with curious eyes and a bloated tummy. A woman from a Georgia rescue organization told me she was found on the side of the road with her mother, a German shepherd. "Momma was skin and bones," she said. I said yes. In the next two weeks, I learned Panda had Parvo. She spent two days in the hospital on IV's, "but she bounced right back," the woman said. I drove four hours with a friend to pick her up. A shelter volunteer placed seven-pound Panda in my arms. She wouldn't stop licking my face. The volunteer said she'd probably be about thirty pounds full-grown.

At home Panda was a terror—biting, howling, ripping anything that she could get her teeth around. Maybe I needed to take her back to Georgia. One friend said, "She's a puppy. Give it a couple years." The first three months involved patience, little sleep and a life-sized stuffed standard poodle—a trainer suggested Panda use that to bite instead of me. But she ripped its tongue off and pulled the stuffing from its mouth. She unearthed plastic toys that Belly buried fifteen years before. The trainer looked at her paws and advised me to get the biggest crate they sell. Scared she might be part Great Dane, I had Panda's DNA tested, which revealed no signs of Border collie. Her daddy was a street dog made up of Dalmation, pit, and boxer.

Maybe I didn't know what was best for me when I checked off the preference boxes on Petfinders and Adoptapet. Or match.com or Tinder. Although the woman who became my long-term partner had a profile on Tinder, I didn't meet her there. She missed my height requirement by an inch.

Four years after bringing Panda home, now at sixty-two pounds, she's all heart. And she could still fit, just barely, through my medium-sized dog door.

THE SECRET LIFE *of* VOLES

To rid the voles killing the ground cover outside my house, I tried castor oil pellets, pinwheels, and sonic devices that beeped once a minute. The voles, or moles, or a combination of the two, dug a network of tunnels, leaving piled up soil mounds resembling little volcanoes. I filled the holes with chewed up bubble gum and coffee grounds—more suggested deterrents to purge the voles. Nothing worked. Yet I kept at it. At times I had been too persistent. Just like I had kept at my search for love using dating apps. Another losing battle. The last woman I had met on a dating app lived two hours away; at first I thought I hit the Tinder jackpot, but on our third date, she drank one beer after the next, a martini to top it off, then stumbled onto my bed and passed out.

Two years prior, I paid a landscaper a thousand bucks to treat the vole-infested area. I called him again, thinking maybe he'd re-treat the area for free, but he said it would cost $2000. The dying Blue Rug Juniper started to overtake the living. Maybe I needed to give it a rest. Perhaps I needed to give my search for love a rest too. But after a few weeks, I'd re-install Tinder or match.com and find myself swiping right or left. Mostly the same heads popped up; they might as well have been moles peeping out into sunlight. Because moles spend most of their lives digging extensive underground tunnel systems, they're nearly blind.

Maybe I would have to make peace by giving up and joining those who are perfectly content without romantic love in their lives. I'd find connection in friends, animals, nature and art.

The voles continued to eat the ground cover roots, so I left the area to die.

But I didn't want to let my heart die. Maybe I was addicted to hope. Yet every time I went back online, I'd get more depressed. Again, I'd give it a rest.

I attempted to ignore the dying shrubs, but they called attention to themselves every time I came and went from my house. So I got in touch with another landscaping company. The estimate to rip out the dead ground cover and redesign the area was $7000 dollars. The cost for internet dating added up as well—monthly fees, anxiety, yoga to relieve anxiety, humiliation, therapy and way too much time.

Maybe I'd have to accept both situations, knowing I tried.

But I went back on OkCupid and continued to search. One local woman popped up. I looked closer. She was married to a man and identified as polyamorous. Thanks but no thanks; I could barely handle myself.

And then I received a message from Luke, who identified as trans-masculine. *I'm just looking for friends*, he wrote. What the hell, I thought. I could use another friend. We exchanged messages about our dogs and favorite hikes. He told me he had worked as a police officer until he injured his back on the job. That's when he started taking hormones and changed his name. Now he worked part-time at a hardware store but wasn't thrilled with the job. He'd much rather be working outside.

With blue-jay eyes, cropped blonde hair and a cleft chin, Luke easily passed as a handsome Southern gentleman. A young Truman Capote. Across a café table, he told me about his girlfriend of five years who left him right after the injury. Ever since, he had bad luck with women, especially the women he met online. "All they want to know," he said, "is what parts I have down there."

"That's just plain rude!" I shook my head and told him about the last woman I had dated, the one who said she didn't have a problem with alcohol.

"I'm so done with these women!" Luke said. "I'm fine with my fur babies. They accept me for who I am."

Maybe we were in the same boat. Perhaps the unconditional love from Panda was enough.

He rubbed his temple, took a sip of soda. "Being out in nature, gardening, digging my hands into soil. That's what makes me happy."

I told Luke about my dead ground covering, the estimate I got for thousands of dollars.

"Whoa!" he said. "Maybe I should take a look."

The next day, Luke surveyed the dried-up Blue Rug Juniper and said he'd be up for the challenge of landscaping the area. He asked for fifteen bucks an hour. I said twenty. He said that was lot more than he got paid at the hardware store. I said not to worry, it had to be cheaper than seven thousand dollars, and together we came up with designs and picked out plants and stones.

Despite his injury, Luke worked his ass off. Some days he worked only two hours, other days seven or eight. He used a chainsaw to break up the thick roots and dragged piles of the dead shrub to the curb for brush pick-up. He carried rocks from one area to another to make retaining walls. He hauled bags of soil from his car, sweat dripping from his shirt and forehead.

OkCupid delivered after all. Or as a friend said, "Maybe in their profiles, people should state what else they do: *Also do plumbing and house-cleaning.*"

"Or maybe," I said, "Luke should have headlined his profile with *Ok Landscape.*"

When Luke needed a break, he sat on my porch, played with my dog, and we talked. I liked hearing stories about his work as a police officer. We shared tales about our families and exes. "I'm done," he said. "Done with these women I'm meeting on line. They're a bunch of liars."

"Most of them are!" I said. "But don't forget, that's where we met."

After twenty years in my small city, I had given up on meeting a love interest nearby. Women either moved here with a partner, or imported a partner they had met online. Although I had good lesbian friends, I didn't feel romantic connections with any; thus, I dated women at a distance. Some across the country. Two who lived in Canada. One in Spain. On paper these women appeared to be good matches, but the relationships all fizzled and I was back sifting through the personals.

Castor oil mixed with dishwashing soap helped deter the voles and moles for a while, but soon enough I'd see soil mounds by mole holes. I learned that voles exploit mole tunnels to get underneath the plants and gnaw at their roots.

A friend suggested I date Luke. "He's handsome," she said, "and he'd have your back and fix things around the house."

Just because someone is a good person and does work around the house doesn't mean I should date them. Although people date others for a lot less.

I did think about the possibility of dating Luke for a second, but my preference was for women on the feminine side of the spectrum. On the other hand, until I was twenty-three, I considered myself straight. Then came along a woman I developed strong feelings for.

Before that, I never thought about gender or sexuality as malleable. I was jealous that my brother got presents that I wanted: toy cars, science sets and fossils. I hated dolls. He was referred to as Dr. Horvitz since a young boy; my career options were limited to a teacher or nurse. In sixth grade, the school guidance counselor said I did well on the English part of the standardized test, but not so well on the science part. "But it's okay," she said. "Science is for boys."

Years ago, while working on a Christmas tree farm in Upstate New York, I met a woman who received a Ph.D. in Plant Biology. As part of her dissertation, she argued that the language of plant terminology is sexist and gendered, making the "male" plant parts aggressors, for example, and "female" parts passive.

After Luke ripped out the dead shrubs, a big pile amassed in front of my house for the city's brush pick up. At the end of the second week, the pile was still there. The sanitation department said they were behind but they'd get to it. Trucks passed without picking the mass up. I phoned again; they said there was too much to pick up and I needed to call a hauling company. "There wouldn't be so much," I said, "if you picked it up in a timely manner." Three weeks later, the gigantic mound became a neighborhood eyesore. After four calls and no action, Luke put on his best Southern gentleman charm and spoke to a sanitation department employee. Later that day, a big white truck clawed up the brush. Luke said, "Thank heavens for men."

Luke lost eight pounds during the two months he worked for me. Not only did he landscape in front of my house, he ripped out invasive ivy covering my backyard and planted a variety of herbs and plants and bushes. And he built two decks in my yard. All the while, we commiserated about women. He told me about a woman he met on OkCupid, and when they met for coffee, he noticed the woman didn't take care of her teeth. "I'm not gonna kiss any girl with black teeth," he said. And then he told me about a woman he chatted with who lived in Boston. "She watched YouTube videos about transgender people," he said, "and went on about all the things she learned from the videos." That infuriated him, but he still drove up north to see her. He came back early. "She just kept making assumptions about what and how I was feeling," he said. "And I told her, she was just damn wrong."

Luke asked my smart speaker, "Alexa, when will I get a date?"

"Hmmm," she said. "I'm not sure."

On his birthday, Luke didn't have plans. I insisted on taking him out for a meal at a local diner. He told me how his sister never called after he had surgery, how his brother basically let his mother die in the worst nursing home in Georgia. "I couldn't do a thing about it," he said. "And when I looked up the ratings of that awful nursing home, it got a 1 out of 5." His head moved side to side. "I loved my Mama," he said.

Two months after meeting Luke, I had once again deleted my dating apps. Internet dating felt like a network of tunnels that led to darkness and pain; yet in the past, it had been a sign of hope, a web of possibilities, or at least an entertaining distraction—what a good friend, in the throes of a recent breakup, needed just then. I helped my heart-broken friend install Tinder on her phone, and within minutes she matched up with local women. Within the hour, she lined up two coffee dates. Over the next few weeks, she went on hikes with new Tinder pals—no one she had interest in dating, but glad to have new buddies, one of whom I met at my friend's birthday party—Kristen.

Tinder markets itself as "more than a dating app. It's a cultural movement." For many, it's about hooking up. For my friend, it was about finding companions to do stuff with. I'd also met women via Tinder when traveling, and we'd meet at Starbucks, have good conversations and friend each other on Facebook. And that was that. A gay male friend mused: "That sounds like the lesbian version of Grinder."

Luke and I talked often. He joined me and a couple friends at a Mexican restaurant to celebrate my birthday. Dressed in a button-down shirt and tie, Luke entertained us with internet dating stories, including the woman he just talked to in Trinidad, who said she wanted to visit Luke—her wife was fine with that. "I told her," Luke said, "I'm *not* fine with that." I told my friends about a woman I had met on match.com: "One of the first things she said to me: 'My number one seat is taken by my daughter, and I'm in her number one seat, and none of that is gonna change until one of us dies.'"

"I tell ya," Luke said. "They're all out of their minds!"

I invited Luke for Thanksgiving. He insisted on making the turkey. I'd never had such a tender turkey. Soon after, he had shoulder surgery. I texted and wrote a long email but didn't hear back.

I worried about him, asked myself why he'd ignore me, if I'd said or done anything that might have offended him.

And spring came and irises and tulips bloomed, along with lavender, oregano, thyme, hummingbird mint, black-eyed Susan, bee balm, milkweed, fern, coneflower, sage—and so did my love life, thanks to Tinder by proxy. Kristen wasn't new to town but new to the lesbian community. She had been married to a man. A couple years ago, she decided to date women. A friend asked, "How could she just decide one day to be a lesbian?" She'd always had crushes on women, figuring all women did.

Kristen, a scientist, gave me a lesson on gender and flowers. She said most flowers are considered hermaphrodite, or—as some call them—bisexual, where the "female" pistil is typically surrounded by the "male" stamens, such as in roses, lilies, and tulips. Perhaps, like flowers, we're all biologically comprised of male and female parts, and the way we express ourselves depends on how those parts speak from within us.

Luke also taught me about flowers, how to care for them, how new growth would come up from old fronds, how I should trim the milkweed back to half. He taught me about gender too, how he'd always felt like a boy, how gender is far from fixed, how finally what he sensed on the inside matched up with his appearance. "I always felt like a freak," he had said. "And now that I'm comfortable in my own body, I can't get myself a date!"

Luke, a perfect combination of what our culture stereotypically considers masculine and feminine, was nurturing, kind, strong and mechanically inclined. When my dog got a bee sting on her paw, he massaged her leg and held her throat, making sure she swallowed a Benadryl. All my friends wanted his number so he could work for them.

After his shoulder surgery, I later learned that Luke turned his phone off and didn't check email. He chose to isolate himself during recovery, not wanting to engage with anyone except a long-time friend, who checked for important emails but accidentally erased mine. She reminded him four months later. I had no idea he had moved three hours away. "It made me sad," he wrote, "to think you'd just disappear."

I told him I missed him and sent a picture of a big red and white hibiscus he planted the year before—wide open and greeting the day.

"That makes me so happy!" he said.

"My yard looks gorgeous," I said, "but twenty percent of the flowers didn't make it. Most likely their roots eaten by the voles."

"Damn those voles!" he said.

As long as I reap the benefits of my labor, I'll continue to search for mole and vole deterrents. One website suggested fox urine pellets, but the reviews slammed the product: "No Good! Attracted more critters!"

Yet I learned an admirable fact about voles: unlike ninety-seven percent of mammals, they're monogamous and often form lifelong unions. I told this to Kristen while we sat on the deck Luke built, overlooking the Blue Ridge Mountains. "They share duties, like raising their babies and making nests," I said. "And one researcher said that if a vole loses a partner, in most cases, it never takes another."

"I'm glad we're not voles," she said. "I'd be stuck in an unhappy marriage."

On my phone, I looked up the lifespan of a vole—three to six months. "Even though they're mostly blind," I said, squeezing Kristen's hand, "they don't have time to blindly search for love."

COMFORTABLE SHOES

ON COUNTLESS OCCASIONS I've been mistaken for a vegetarian. My response has been, "I like meat. Bloody, drippy meat," a comment stolen from my college boyfriend. He had yelled at a Hare Krishna who asked if we'd like to come to a free vegetarian dinner. Both of us dressed in jeans, tie-dyed t-shirts, and bandanas on our heads, my boyfriend added, "You picked the wrong people to mess with!" The orange-robed man sprinted away. The truth is, I'm sickened by blood and prefer my meat cooked well.

I tried to figure out why I've taken offense at this assumption, why I felt it necessary to be provocative. What it comes down to, I suspect, is my internalized homophobia. Because I wear comfortable shoes, a fleece jacket and a buff on my head, one might suspect I'm a lesbian, and the stereotype, at least when I struggled to come out, was (and still is in some circles) that lesbians are vegetarians. In an attempt to mitigate the lesbian assumption, a friend said, "You could be an earthy, hippie, granola type." Even if I look like a hybrid of the two—an earthy, hippie, crunchy lesbian—I wanted to drive the point home that tofu is not necessarily my homeboy.

In my mind, when someone said, "I could have sworn you were a vegetarian," I might as well have heard, "You're a lesbian, and lesbians are vegetarians. And lesbians are ugly man-hating women with bad haircuts who are too ugly to get a guy." A child of the seventies, I knew of no out lesbians while growing up. Zero.

Not if you don't count Billie Jean King, who was forced to come out of the closet in 1981; as a result she lost all of her endorsements. So if lesbians did exist, they had to hide, erase themselves.

In the late eighties, a friend from college, Jenny, visited me in Manhattan. She told me about her new boyfriend. She asked about our mutual friends—who had a new boyfriend, who was now single. I gave her updates. She never asked about my life. And because she never asked, I assumed she knew she knew about my girlfriend. If she had asked, I would have told her. Was she only trying to protect me, thinking that she'd spare me from revealing a shameful secret that obviously wasn't meant to be a secret? She continued to ask about friends. I wanted to scream. I hated her for not asking. But I hated myself more for not telling. Why was I playing this stupid game, which only made me complicit with Jenny and everyone else who thought there was something wrong with me?

It didn't help that the AIDS crisis was in full swing, and even though lesbians were the least likely group to transmit the virus, the mainstream viewed all homosexuals as pariahs. The president at the time, Ronald Reagan, said society could not "condone" the "alternative" gay "lifestyle." Before he publicly uttered the word "AIDS," over 12,000 Americans had died of the virus. The late Senator Jesse Helms declared that "homosexuals and lesbians [are] disgusting people marching in our streets demanding all sorts of things, including the right to marry each other," and that they are "weak, morally sick wretches."

Comforted when I spent time with my straight guy friends, I referred to them as my "surrogate boyfriends." I could feel "normal" in the company of an adoring male, even if I had no interest in them romantically. They gladly escorted me to lesbian bars. One night my friend Ron accompanied me to The Cubbyhole, a corner bar in the West Village. An inebriated friend, Kiki, chatted me up, but when Ron laughed along with us, she flicked a lit cigarette at him.

Even though attitudes have changed, my homophobia runs deep. And it's not just me. A friend of mine pointed out that in restaurants, we always get seated at the "lesbian table," a table in back by the bathroom (and sometimes by the slamming kitchen door). I noticed this too. To prove it to another friend, the next time we went out, the hostess led us to the back by the bathrooms, passing by a number of empty tables. I asked if we could sit in a better location. She sighed and seated us up front. The theory behind the "lesbian table" is that unconsciously (or perhaps not) the hostess pegs us as lesbians. Historically, lesbians haven't had much money (women haven't had much money!) and dress in frumpy attire, so the hostess hides us in back, out of the way. But we've already spent too much time in hiding.

My hairdresser said half of her clientele are lesbians, and many tell her not to give them a lesbian haircut.

"What's a lesbian haircut?" I asked.

"You know," she said, "the faux-hawk, with short spiky hair gelled to the front."

Back in the eighties, the popular haircut of the time was the mullet. I had one. Yet the mullet continued to be popular in the lesbian community. In the early nineties, I got my mullet cut into a pixie, and even though I no longer had to contend with my thick Jewish hair, my girlfriend at the time said I looked like Phranc—a self-described "All-American Jewish lesbian folksinger," who had a flattop haircut. I didn't want to look like her. I had a hard enough time embracing my Jewishness. I hated my last name, thought it was too Jewish. I cringed when I had to say it aloud, or when teachers called my name in class. They rarely got it right. But even with the correct pronunciation, I associated Jewishness with my father, who yelled across restaurants to get the waitress's attention, and my mother, who filled her pocketbook with leftover breadsticks and butter sachets, and counted pennies after receiving change.

I envied the quiet blonde kids, the "Christians" as my father referred to them. I wanted silky blonde hair and a normal family that spoke in hushed tones in restaurants.

My father, who grew up in the Midwest, told stories about kids calling him a kike, asking if he had horns, and during his stint in the army during World War II, other soldiers called him a dirty Jew.

I had run-ins with anti-Semitism too. In junior high, I told the girl sitting behind me in homeroom that my grandfather was a rabbi. The next day she asked to see my rubber eraser. She returned it with the word "Whore" penned across it. That same day, a gang of girls, led by the girl from homeroom, pushed me against a row of lockers and called me a dirty Jew. I shoved one of them back across the hall and ran. When they saw my brother later that day, they said, "Tell your sister to beware." Yet they didn't bother me again.

Probably a reaction to coming of age during the Depression era (and their parents escaping poverty in Eastern Europe), my parents created a culture of scarcity around food. We fought over who got what chicken part, who got to gnaw on the steak bone, and who got more meatballs with their spaghetti. Although my parents had money to afford enough food for their four kids, they came home from the grocery store with half-price items such as almost moldy bread and dented cans. The way food was treated in my family reminded me of a film I'd later see of Jews sneaking carrots and cucumbers under their shirts into the Warsaw Ghetto.

In my late twenties, I visited the Warsaw Ghetto, Auschwitz and Birkenau, and the stark reality of the Holocaust hit me.

On my way back to the train station, a Swedish man walked with me. "It would be better," he said, "to honor the dead if they razed the buildings and made this area into a big beautiful green field."

I stopped in my tracks. "People need to be reminded," I said, "that the Holocaust really happened."

"There could be a plaque," the blonde man said, "to remind people of the event."

"You can't remind people of the event, or honor the dead," I said, "by hiding the evidence."

I began to embrace my Jewish identity after visiting Auschwitz. If I had been born four or fives decades earlier, I could have been the target of violent attacks and handed over to authorities by my neighbors. I could have been dehumanized, referred to as a disease-carrying rat, similar to the Hutus involved in the Rwanda genocide, who referred to the Tutsis as cockroaches.

Since then, when asked if I'm entirely Jewish, I say, "100% and proud."

Some theorize that women, and perhaps lesbians in particular, are more sympathetic to animal rights, since they've experienced oppression, what it means to be denied basic human rights. Jane Velez-Mitchell, author of *Addict Nation*, echoes this sentiment: "The lesbian community knows what it's like to be voiceless and to be treated as 'less than.' That's why we often have exceptional empathy for the downtrodden, the overlooked, the forgotten."

Although mainstream culture has slowly embraced the LGBTQ population, I still feel uneasy holding hands with my girlfriend. She came out a few years ago and doesn't fully understand my concerns. She didn't have to contend with the homophobic world I grew up in, the world where all I wanted to do was fit in, to be normal, and normal, for me, meant being blonde, straight, Christian, and meat-eating.

These days, vegetarians are not limited to old stereotypes of spacey waifs, Hare Krishnas, and cropped-haired lesbians in flannel doddering through food co-op aisles. According to a *Time* article, 25% of adolescents consider vegetarianism "cool." And some might even think lesbianism is cool too. A majority of my female students of late identify as queer.

Just the other day, a model-pretty blonde sat next to me on a flight from New York to Charlotte. She had rushed onto the plane, clutching a Styrofoam to-go cup from the airport bar. She said she had spent the weekend with her sorority sisters from college but had a husband and young child back home. She asked where I was from.

"I love Asheville!" she said. "I did a yoga retreat there!"

She taught yoga. She worked for a Republican think-tank. When the airline attendant came around, she asked if she could buy me a drink. I had a scotch. She asked if I was seeing anyone. I said I had a girlfriend and showed her a picture of Kristen. "She's adorable," the woman said. "I think I'm a lesbian. Women are so much smarter. Really, maybe I'm a lesbian."

Despite her inebriation, I doubt this conversation would have happened ten years ago. Since when was it cool to be a lesbian?

"Your girlfriend is hot," the woman said.

Kristen is mostly vegetarian. Since she's met me, she said, she's eaten more meat but wants to cut down. And I've been eating less.

"But haven't people," I asked Kristen, "been eating meat for millennia?"

Tens of thousands of years ago, she told me, humans ate everything they could get a hold of. If they could catch an animal, they gorged themselves on it before it went bad. Now food is easy to come by, so we can make better choices. "Eating meat," she said, "is bad for the world. Besides the animal abuse, farming animals takes a huge toll on the environment—think about the loss of water, soil, trees. Anyone who calls themselves an environmentalist and eats meat is a hypocrite."

I lowered my head, wishing I had heard about slaughterhouses while in grade school. After all, I learned about slavery and the Holocaust. I learned about the consequences of smoking and saw images of blackened lungs and sickly old people gasping by oxygen tanks. I learned how a cow's udders provide milk. Although I'm cutting down on my meat intake and only buy organic, I still consume it.

On a recent blustery day in downtown Asheville, Kristen and I held hands. My curly locks blew in all directions. She said, "You've got such great hair. It's got a life of its own!" A gang of high school kids ambled down the street in our direction. I slowly tugged my hand away. But before the group passed, I placed my hand back in hers and squeezed it and forced myself to keep it there. A girl in the group, wearing a red baseball cap and torn jeans, lingered behind, looking down, singing to herself. When she looked up, we locked eyes. She half-smiled, looked down again, then ran to catch up with her friends.

ONE WITHERING ROSE

Even though I hadn't seen her, or barely talked to my college friend Tami over the past four years, I organized a Zoom memorial for her. After all, we were in the middle of a pandemic, and no one else took the lead, and her parents were dead, and her ex was dead, and her sister was dead, and her twenty-year-old son acted as if his mother's death was a minor inconvenience—a result, I suspect, of shock, grief, or perhaps anger. After all, Tami drank herself to death.

I set up a Facebook invite, and a couple days later, twenty-three digitized rectangles of old friends from college, summer camp, elementary and junior high school, showed up. Most hadn't been in touch with Tami for over a decade. We spoke about the Tami we once knew, the topnotch illustrator who worked in the comic industry, but once work dried up, a decade before, she hadn't worked again. Friends talked about her biting wit, her immense talent. One woman told the story of Tami contacting a rabbi to perform her son's circumcision at emoil.com. After the procedure, she buried the foreskin, wrapped up in a handkerchief, in a random planter on Fifth Avenue. I spoke about how we grew up together as young adults. We met at seventeen, both of us art students living in a college suite of hippie girls. What I didn't have time to say: with our suitemates, we traveled to an outdoor Grateful Dead show in Lewiston, Maine in a piss-colored Datsun B-210; we took the train from our college just north of Manhattan to eat at Wo-Hops on

Mott Street, and to see Simon and Garfunkel play Central Park. In our suite, I played guitar and we sang Joni Mitchell and Neil Young songs and together we wrote a song, "Feeling Skeevy," poking fun at our girlfriends who dated lots of men. The chorus: "And you woke up next to me / and I wondered if I had VD / and you know it's probably true / everybody knows about you / They say you're really skeevy / but now I'm skeevy too." On my twentieth birthday, Tami organized a surprise party for me, and I was truly surprised. She baked a delicious birthday cake for the event, topped off by magic relighting candles.

We both moved to the East Village after graduation and explored Little Italy and Chinatown, and we hung out at the Life Café on Tenth Street and Avenue B, where I first saw Eileen Myles read her poetry. We befriended a group of guys to hang out with on weekends, including one who knew of at least two parties every night. Sometimes we'd hear music and see a crowd of people dancing through a tenement window, and we'd buzz the buzzer and crash the party. Tami and I competed for who could get the most phone numbers from guys in bars, and by the end of the night, we'd have a pocket full of paper scraps. We saw Rickie Lee Jones singing on a Manhattan Pier overlooking the Hudson, and Jones was drunk or high and screamed at the audience when someone told her to quit drinking. Tami witnessed my transition from straight to bi to lesbian and encouraged me through my coming out struggles. She accompanied me to West Village lesbian bars, and late at night we'd walk back to the East Village while we sang Cyndi Lauper songs. She said she always had crushes on women but had it in her head she'd marry a man.

And she did marry a man she met at a bar across from her apartment on East Third Street, next to the Hell's Angel's Headquarters. Before she said yes, she asked if I thought she was making the right decision. "Are you in love with him?" I asked. "I'm not sure," she said. "But he looks really good on paper."

Two years after I moved to Asheville, she gave birth. We made plans to get together the next time I visited New York, but I bailed. Accompanied by a new girlfriend who'd never been to Manhattan, I was excited to play tour guide, show off my old stomping grounds. But the new girlfriend threatened to take the next plane home soon after we landed. She said the city was too crowded and noisy and too many people were mentally ill and asked how I could have lived in such a disgusting place for so long and she needed a drink. I could barely manage the girlfriend, let alone visit Tami and her infant. I apologized profusely, but Tami cut me off. I reached out through email with no response.

Maybe she felt I abandoned her when she needed me most. Was our friendship that precarious? Perhaps she wasn't such a good friend. Years before, she had attempted to date a man she knew I had a big crush on while I was out of town. When I returned and asked if she'd seen him, she hemmed and hawed. The man, with whom I later had a romance, said Tami kept calling him. My long-term college boyfriend also told me that Tami tried to seduce him one night. Although I never mentioned these friendship breaches, I forgave her.

Yet she didn't forgive me. Not until eight years later, when she sent an email to let me know about her impending divorce. "You were the only one," she said, "who told me to think twice before marrying him." Happy to have her back in my life, I didn't question why she cut me off. After that email, we'd get together when I visited New York, but now she gazed off in the distance and chain-smoked. She talked about her ex's drinking, how she asked him for a copy of his tax returns to help her apply for her son's camp scholarship. "He dropped off the tax returns and before he left," she said, "he pried the mezuzah off my door." I told her about my foray into long-distance internet dating because of Asheville's limited pool of women. She talked of her own dating prospects: "I'm old, not that pretty, I smoke and drink, and I'm unemployed and have a child. Who the hell would want me?"

I told Tami she looked great, that she hadn't aged since college, that she was smart, funny and talented.

A year later, Tami's ex drank himself to death. "What an asshole," she said. "He had to kill himself three months after our divorce was finalized? Now I lose my health insurance."

I saw Tami a couple more times; once she insisted on meeting at a Penn Station bar, where she ordered a jumbo Bloody Mary. The last time we met up, she suggested a narrow steamy bakery. She was depressed; she didn't know what she was doing with her life. I suggested she find a therapist, join Meetup, quit smoking. She changed the subject to our college days. I mentioned my college boyfriend who I dated for five years. "I tried to Google him," I said. "I couldn't find a thing. Maybe he's dead."

Tami had no recollection of him.

"How could you not remember?" I asked. "We all hung out together!"

"I got nothing," she said, looking off in the distance.

I wondered if her marriage traumatized her to the point of wiping out her memory. Not until the day before she passed, when she was in a coma, did I learn about her heavy drinking.

Following our encounter at the bakery, she always had an excuse as to why she couldn't meet, unless I wanted to come up to her Upper East Side tenement, which I'd been to once. Dark and reeking of cigarette smoke and kitty litter, I begged to meet in the middle, offered to take her out to a nice restaurant, but after too many excuses, I stopped asking.

On Facebook, she had posted pictures of her son, old comic strips, and elaborate meals she cooked. From the digital life she presented, Tami appeared to be doing fine. I later learned from the only friend she'd been in regular contact with that she never actually ate those meals. She also posted about the falls she took in front of her building and how clumsy she was. The last time she fell, she never got up.

During our Zoom memorial, I told the group of pixelated faces about a strange occurrence—after I had posted the Facebook invite, a sweet smell wafted through my house. Roses maybe. The scent became stronger and stronger. I walked around, trying to figure out where the smell had come from. Definitely roses. My gut reaction—this was Tami's thank you for setting up the memorial. Within minutes, the smell dissipated.

"That doesn't surprise me," a friend of hers said. "She loved flowers. The last time we hung out, I drove her to a florist to pick up roses."

A woman from her building said, "She was on the building's flower committee. That was her pride and joy."

I had no idea about Tami's love of flowers. Perhaps since I had last seen her, flowers helped brighten up her dark days. I'm glad something brought her joy.

In the distant past, before the dead were embalmed, flowers masked the odor of a decomposing body; the fragrance hid the smell long enough for the funeral to take place. Now I imagine Tami in her apartment alone, slowly dying during the pandemic, a bouquet of flowers nearby, all the while clicking away on Facebook, masking her pain behind a digital persona.

But I also imagine Tami as she was once, as we once were together—two twenty-something fresh-faced women strolling down St. Mark's Place, or sitting in the Odessa Diner on Avenue A. We'd order potato perogis and kasha with gravy and talk about boys and girls and traveling the world, when we would never think of buying flowers—they'd die too soon, when our futures were an exciting unknown.

THE STORY *of a* MIRROR

I WASN'T EXACTLY LOOKING FOR A SHAMAN to clear my house of ghosts, but over dinner I learned that a friend's new partner, Debby, had studied shamanism. I told Debby about the orbs I'd seen in the past, the sweet aromas that suddenly permeated my living room and disappeared just as swiftly, and the shadowy figure that appeared multiple times by my bed when I had woken in the middle of the night. I told Debby about two shamans who had come to my house four years earlier, after I returned from a vacation in Greece. Before I left, I could barely sleep. For three weeks straight. In Greece I slept fine.

One shaman had studied in Peru. She lit sage and said prayers in each room while my dog, without my knowledge, chewed up the shaman's sandals. The other shaman spit something called Florida Water into the corners of my bedroom and told me to get plants and more furniture. (Three years later, the spitter was a student in my creative writing class, but we never acknowledged that she came to my house and cast demons out with her saliva. But she did complain to me in an email about the younger students, one who got defensive and left early after the shaman told her, during a peer critique, that the student's poetry was full of clichés. "I've got my own clichés to deal with," the shaman said.)

Now Debby asked, "Did they help you sleep better?"

"They did," I said, "but I still feel a weird energy in my house."

A few days later, Debby toured my home. I followed her into my bedroom, where she closed her eyes and took a deep breath. I looked into the wall mirror and saw myself—a middle-aged woman in a gray T-shirt, the worry lines on my face deepening. A mirror an ex brought back from Mexico over twenty years before. A mirror that had seen me transform from an insecure mess who tolerated that ex's false accusations, including a claim that I was still in love with my ex before her, and that I was selfish because I didn't ask for, or want, a bed she commissioned her friend to build for me. I had since gotten rid of the bed. Maybe I needed to get rid of the mirror.

Debby said she felt a heavy energy in my bedroom. "Do you want to know what I sensed?"

I nodded.

"A dark-haired soldier was hung on your property," she said. "He needs to be taken home to the upper world to be with his ancestors."

That creeped me out but also explained the shadowy figure moving like a time-lapse image by my bed. I'd be scared out of my mind and say loudly, "Hello?" And turn the light on and tell myself the shadows were only part of a dream.

"Before I clear your house," Debby said, "I need to help you clear the stuck energy inside of you, and the grief from your mother's death."

A week later, I lay on a massage table in Debby's living room, where she used a drum, rattles, stones, feathers, wind and a crystal bowl to clear my energy. I tried to let go of the cynical part of me that thought this ritual was ridiculous. A white woman blowing on my forehead, performing a ritual appropriated from Indigenous culture, while frantic drumming blared from her iPhone.

Debby and I sat on her couch to debrief. She said she unblocked most of my grief. She had visions of a young child reaching out but never quite grabbing hold of another hand. "Does that make sense?" she asked.

I told her about my mother, how I longed for her attention. Reaching out but never grabbing hold.

Debby said my spirit animal is a butterfly: "It's all about transformation and becoming lighter. And more colorful. Give your house more color. Wear more colorful clothing."

Five days later, Debby tapped on a handheld drum and walked through each room in my house. I followed behind, holding up and blowing on a stick of burning sage. Outside, we burned pieces of different plants I gathered, making up colors of the rainbow. Debby pointed out the crows flying by a nearby tree. "That's a good sign," she said. "They're here to help us."

She said the soldier spirit in my bedroom had crossed over to the upper world.

Later that day, a friend asked if I believed what the shaman said about the soldier spirit.

"I believe the shaman believes it," I said. "I want to believe her. I want to believe she cleared out my house. And my stuck grief. And sometimes I do. Maybe believing is enough."

My friend told me about Marie Condo's rules for clearing out one's house: "Discard anything that doesn't spark joy. And if you have a hard time getting rid of something, you need to ask yourself: Am I having trouble getting rid of this because of an attachment to the past or because of a fear for the future?" Because my mother was a hoarder, I've been well aware of needing to keep my house sparse, of feeling the weight of clutter. After over twenty years in the same place, I took inventory of what didn't bring me joy. First was the mirror in my bedroom given to me by the accusatory ex. I took it off the wall and started a pile of stuff I would donate to Goodwill.

Even my Gmail inbox held stuck energy. I had over 6000 messages, mainly from women I met through dating websites. What had I been holding onto? I started deleting messages, hundreds of them at a time. Yet I didn't delete emails from two friends who died, both of cancer. I wanted to hold onto their words, to their memories, to the laughter we shared.

After my mother's sudden death, I helped my father clear out bags upon bags of coupons and decades upon decades of receipts and maps and birthday cards. I loaded them in giant trash bags and put them to the curb. I remember the piles of newspapers and magazines my mother kept in her bedroom. Did she ever read them?

What I do believe: possessions and homes hold energy. That's why I've always been scared of old houses, ancient furniture, and walking through antique shops. The amassed energy makes me anxious.

Now it was time to clear away the energy of the ex-girlfriend who gave me the mirror, and the younger version of myself who looked in that mirror—the same version of myself that got a jolt when I received yet another email from an internet woman, the version of myself that could turn off communication with the click of a switch, the version of myself that felt safer from a distance in order to safeguard myself from the hurt of abandonment and heartache.

As soon as I dropped off the mirror and bags of clothes at Goodwill, I felt lighter. I bought a mirror at Target. While there, I tried on a colorful blouse of printed flowers. I liked it. I liked me in it. I paid for it and wore it out of the store. Maybe it was time to let go and embrace my spirit animal, to add colors to my drab wardrobe, to flitter among flowers and feel as weightless and decorated as butterfly wings.

I REMEMBER YOU, ALLEN GINSBERG

I REMEMBER YOU DRESSED in your signature gray suit and tie, sitting behind a desk in a mint green classroom, when I cowered into the room and introduced myself. "We need to set up a meeting time," I said. "You're my tutorial instructor." You patted the seat next to you. I sat down and told you that part of me felt like I didn't belong in the MFA Program—I wasn't an undergraduate English major; I had a BFA in photography. You said, "I'm a photographer too!" and proceeded to show me a book of your photographs, turning each page, your scribbly descriptions below, including the famous one of Jack Kerouac smoking a cigarette on a fire escape, taken on East Seventh Street, the same street I lived on, in a walkup tenement flat, above a Polish shoe repair/travel agency.

Twenty-seven years later, while going through boxes of old photos and journals, I came across the *New York Times* clipping of your obituary: *Allen Ginsberg, Master Poet of Beat Generation, Dies at 70*. When you died in 1997, I was thirty-five, in the last year of an English doctoral program, for which you wrote a recommendation letter (you asked me to write the letter myself and you'd "Ginsberg-ize it"). At the time of your death, seventy seemed old; you lived a long and productive life.

But now I stared at the twenty-three year-old obituary. Only seventy? You died way too young!

This past semester, I taught a course I first took with you in 1993, four years before your death: Writers of the Beat Generation. In your class, we started with a short meditation, and your buddies made guest appearances: Gregory Corso, always considered the jokester, asked us what was on the cover of his book, *The Happy Birthday of Death* (it looked like clouds and stars at night). "That's my sperm!" he said. And Gary Snyder, the Buddhist who didn't seem all that spiritual as he gawked at the women in class, and Peter Orlovsky, the love of your life—an overweight, quiet man.

Allen, I want to tell you my students loved you. They found inspiration in your words and actions; they got a kick out of the video of you playing your harmonium and chanting Hare Krishna while grinning at conservative talk-show host William S. Buckley. I loved how you disarmed him, how you disarmed the world with your words.

You were only seventy when you died in your apartment, surrounded by friends. And now your age of death jolted me. Only seventy! My friend Lisa, with whom I hitchhiked up and down the California coast at eighteen, is now dating a seventy year-old, a bearded hippie Santa Claus. Back then we'd get into cars with men who offered us marijuana. Since Lisa's birthday was five days before mine, I'd say, "We were conceived at the same moment!" And the drivers would say, "What were your parents doing together?"

As I reach the end of my fifties, seventy is quickly approaching. How did I get here so fast? How did you get there so fast?

In that mint green classroom, you read my poetry, and in one poem I wrote about my father, how he handled the raging battles between his parents: "I sat in the closet and read the dictionary." You asked if that was true, and I said yes, and you said, "That's pretty funny." You told me to delete extraneous words, like "the" and "a," and encouraged me to write haiku-like poems. You especially praised me for this one:

WARNING
Xeroxed Sign
Grainy photo of Middle-Eastern man
Magic-markered
"Do not give this man a cat"
hangs on wall
in Korean deli.

I remember you said it's okay to experiment with my sexuality. At the time I had a girlfriend but was closeted. You said you slept with men and women in your younger years. "That's the only way," you said, "to figure it out." And then you said, "Now that I've got a lot of money, I can't even get it up." I loved how you blurted out whatever came into your mind, your irreverence, your famous quote, "First thought, best thought."

Your life-long friend, William Burroughs, said of your life: "He stood for freedom of expression and for coming out of all the closets long before others did. He has influence because he said what he believed."

During my first semester of grad school, my peers in their early twenties rolled their eyes when talking about you, happy they didn't have to work with you, how they'd heard you gave little attention to female students. But I didn't feel neglected during our one-on-one meetings. Another student mentioned that school administrators had recently scolded you about this. Clearly I benefitted from this reprimand, although I did observe you doodling during a student reading while female classmates presented their poetry; yet, you were attentive when pretty boys read their work. I mentioned this in a paper I presented at a Beat Conference, and Joyce Johnson, Kerouac's girlfriend when *On the Road* came out, and author of the memoir, *Minor Characters*, said she could tell me hundreds of similar stories.

This semester, a few students accused the Beats of misogyny, particularly Kerouac and Burroughs. I agreed, but said they should be given a little leeway. Yes, the Beat Generation was a boy's club, and yes, you and Burroughs and Kerouac had revolutionary ideas about freedom of expression and challenging the status quo, but when it came to gender equality, you had your blind spots. Yet all of us have been steeped in sexism and neatly defined gender roles. A couple women singled out Kerouac's *On the Road*, but I reminded them that the book was written in 1949, to put it in cultural and historical context. Besides, Kerouac was an insecure and broken man, always running back to his mother. He drank himself to death at forty-seven. Despite the sexist accusations, a few women fell in love with Kerouac through his writing, and like Joyce Johnson, would have bought him a hot dog and leant him money and invited him to crash at their apartment.

My friend Jan gave me her copy of *Minor Characters* the semester I started sharing my poetry with you. While re-reading the book for my class this past semester, I thought of Jan. We both had worked as graphic artists at an Irish American Newspaper, located across from the Empire State Building. We kept up with each other for a decade, but when she moved to Woodstock, we lost touch. Now I found her on Facebook and wrote to her, asked how she was doing and thanked her for giving me her copy of *Minor Characters*. She wrote back and said she didn't remember the book, but she remembered me. "You just started grad school," she said, "and studied with Allen Ginsberg. And by the way," she said, "I have a twenty-five year-old son." And just like that, a full-grown man appeared. Like magic. A generation come and gone.

Allen, I've been teaching college ever since we met every Thursday night at Brooklyn College for our one-on-one meetings, when we cabbed it back to the East Village together, when I knew our teacher/student sessions were a gift, when I was shy and nervous and listened to your stories and giggled, when I hadn't known exactly how much of a difference you made in the world of poetry and politics and social consciousness. I knew you were an icon, I knew you wrote "Howl" and controversy surrounded its publication, but you were so much more than that. In your 1956 poem "America," you put your "queer shoulder to the road," long before any queers even uttered the word, let alone announced it to the world.

Twenty-three years after your death, during the pandemic, my students read "America," and wrote updated versions of the poem. One started off his poem: "America, when will this virus end? The Covid-19 virus, the Trump virus. The racist virus. America, are you listening?" We talked about similarities between Trump values and the Red Scare in the late 40's and early 50's, when, as you said of that era, "...you had completely false set of values being presented in terms of morality, ethics and success: the man of distinction....You had the aggression of the closet queen J. Edgar Hoover and the alcoholic, intemperate Senator McCarthy working together..." McCarthy's right hand man, Roy Cohn, mentored Trump, advised him to never admit defeat. Cohn, on his deathbed, dying of AIDS, adamantly denied his homosexuality; if he did, apparently, he would have admitted defeat.

But you, Allen, had no problem calling hypocrites out and embracing your authentic self. You had no problem speaking about your sexual relationship with hyper-masculine, womanizer Neal Cassady. You even professed your love to Kerouac, who, according to historians, had his own homoerotic encounters, most likely with Cassady as well—Kerouac's long-time obsession and muse.

It took years to fully embrace my queerness, my Jewishness, and for the first time, when teaching this past semester's Beat Generation class, I said, "My partner, she...," and felt liberated in doing so. Back in the 80's and early 90's, too scared, too closeted to march in the Gay Pride Parade in New York, I stood on the sidelines and cheered, envied those who could dance and smile and wave to the crowds. Even at Greenwich Village lesbian bars, I felt safer when I brought my straight guy friends, perhaps to protect me from being a full-on lesbian.

Allen, you and other Beat writers paved the way for civil rights, the anti-war movement, LGBTQ rights, even women's rights. Amiri Baraka, the most prominent Black writer associated with the Beats, commented, "I took up with the Beats because that's what I saw taking off and flying somewhere resembling myself. The open and implied rebellion—of form and content....I could see the young white boys and girls in their pronouncements of disillusion with and "removal" from society as related to the black experience. That made us colleagues of the spirit."

You spoke your mind, Allen, when others feared for their safety, when "normal" meant moving to the suburbs and living a quiet life.

I didn't know it at the time, but I connected with Beat writing because I also experimented, took risks, and always liked a good challenge—I opened my heart to a variety of romances, quit good jobs to travel the world, and as a photo major, played with multiple exposures, transparent images and used paint and mixed media. One classmate, a boy who made technically perfect prints of houses and flowers, said, "What's wrong with a pretty picture?"

Allen, you said, "Poetry should make trouble." I wanted to make trouble, to say something new. When I showed my mother my experiments, she said, "What ever happened to those nice sunsets you used to take pictures of?" Pretty pictures are safe. I wanted more out of life than safety. I wanted to challenge the viewer, to challenge myself. My mother, an undergrad art major, married and moved to the suburbs. The suburbs were safe, marriage was safe, but both, I suspect, shut off the valve to her artistic expression.

You said, "Follow your inner moonlight; don't hide the madness. You say what you want to say when you don't care who's listening." And you did just that.

At seventy, on your deathbed, you went through your phonebook and called your friends to say goodbye. At thirty-five, I was sad to hear of your death and saved your obituary clipping, but now, finding that news-clipping affected me in a profound way, especially after spending a semester talking about you, how much of a father figure you became to Beat children, how you exuded joy and calmness.

Although I taught the course before, I took a five-year hiatus from it. Half a decade ago, loudmouths in the class got on the "all the Beats are misogynist" bandwagon and remained there for the entirety of the class (unlike this past semester). One student said, "*On the Road* would never be published today." Another student said, "It's offensive. We shouldn't have to read such sexist crap." I explained that sexist books get published all the time, but it's important to look at the context, to think about Kerouac's breakthrough writing style, why the book is still revered.

The conflict between "politically correct" culture and freedom of speech began to explode within the last decade, especially at liberal arts colleges. Some warned of suppression of speech, while others welcomed the shift toward a more sensitive culture. But I felt bullied by the loudmouths; I had to tread carefully, no longer able to engage with certain texts, fearing the wrath of students who felt "offended" or "uncomfortable." What the hell happened, Allen? Isn't discomfort where the real learning takes place? The irony here is that you championed free speech and freedom of the press, and in that class, students actively engaged in censorship and shutting down dialogue. I suspect you'd be horrified by this behavior. I suspect you'd give these students a talking to, tell them to buck up, challenge themselves, to let their minds expand.

But this time around, my students, inspired by you and your buddies, brought passion into our discussions, connected the urgency of your words with the Black Lives Matter movement and other contemporary issues. They had no idea how much the Beats had an impact on popular culture, how Burroughs inspired the grunge and punk movements, how you and Bob Dylan were buddies, how the FBI followed you because they feared your pacifist actions might work.

One student said, "I am inspired by Allen Ginsberg, and think about the first line of 'Howl' at least once every few days. His poetry not only inspired my writing, but a deep dive into knowledge of myself and what I truly want out of life." Another said, "The image of a bright sunflower covered in soot portrayed in Ginsberg's 'Sunflower Sutra' inspires me to see my future high school students as bright yellow sunflowers and inspire them to think outside the box."

On the last day of class, I told my students I hadn't taught the course in five years because I needed a break. But by bringing so much enthusiasm to each session, they made me fall in love with the Beats again, especially you, Allen. They helped me see why we needed their words and actions to stir things up in the 50's and 60's, and why we need them, more than ever, now.

VICTORY LAP

During the first year of COVID-19, I devised and taught a first year college seminar: Queer Arts/Queer Activism, combining my passion for art, social justice and queer history. In a time of forced isolation, my students, already part of a generation riddled with anxiety, were not only stuck in their rooms but in their heads. We all needed a release, but the quarantine was especially hard on students who left home for the first time and struggled to make sense of their queer identities. Before the pandemic, most felt a sense of isolation already too familiar in a homophobic world. I know that feeling all too well.

A good majority of students lived in the college dorms (even though a major portion of classes were remote). They left their rooms, socially distanced and masked, only to pick up boxed meals from the cafeteria.

After years of struggling to make sense of my own identity, I finally felt comfortable enough, finally had the confidence to lead discussions on queer representation through art. So there I was, the self-assured professor in my Zoom rectangle. On my screen, student faces filled eighteen rectangles, their bunk beds and, at times, roommates, appeared in the background.

Little did they know, for a good part of my life, especially growing up in a chaotic family, I didn't feel seen or heard, so I isolated myself in my hot pink bedroom. Since kindergarten, I went to school with the same kids who sensed an easy target, like a sixth-grade classmate, who asked to see the handheld fan I brought to class. When she gave it back, she smelled her hand, as if it soaked up whatever rot dripped off mine.

Yet creating art saved me, kept me afloat when I otherwise would have drowned in a sea of loneliness. Art has continued to save me through heartache and trauma.

With my freshman class, we talked about how societal pressure to conform beat famous people down, like Whitney Houston, who had a long-term relationship with Robyn Crawford. They met as teenagers. When Houston signed her record contract, she told Crawford that they couldn't be physical. In her memoir, Crawford wrote, "If people found out, they would use this against us, and back in the 80's, that's how it felt." Four years after Houston's suicide, Bobby Brown, Houston's ex-husband, said, "I really feel that if Robyn was accepted into Whitney's life, Whitney would still be alive today." Who knows how many queer lives have been ruined because they got sent off by their families for shock treatments, married someone they didn't love, or were (and still are) forced to go to ex-gay ministry camps and conversion therapies.

Even in this time when queers can marry, when we have a plethora of positive queer role models, subtle and not so subtle messages about conforming to the status quo remain loud and clear. By discussing art made by self-identified queer artists, students could see their own identities reflected back. For example, after analyzing a photograph, a student responded: "... it seems to represent the isolation and loneliness that many queer individuals go through...I can relate to this because when I was still (and still am) figuring myself out I didn't really know anyone I could talk to about being different. This picture shows a sense of mental isolation as well. Even when you're surrounded by a bunch of people, you still feel just as alone."

Although I didn't discover my own queerness until I was in my twenties, and didn't know much about queer history until much later, now I led a discussion about two transgender activists who were on the frontlines of the Stonewall Riots: Sylvia Rivera, who was Latina, and Marsha P. Johnson, who was black, when gay or gender non-conforming people faced the possibility of arrest, even in New York City. Students watched a documentary about Harvey Milk, who most knew nothing about. One student responded to the film: "I've never heard of him and I'm so upset that I hadn't. He seemed like such a sweet man. He was inclusive, caring, smart, and altogether seemed like a great person to have in a position of power."

All of my students chose to be in this class; all identified as queer. Some were light years ahead of others when it came to articulating concepts like intersectionality; as an eighteen-year-old, I could barely string a sentence together, let alone talk about abolitionist theory. Then again, I grew up in a different time, a different generation, when the idea of trans-rights, gay marriage and gender non-binary were not yet concepts.

A week into my freshman year, in the campus pub, my roommate and I tried to acquire the taste of Budweiser. For the first time I felt an alcohol buzz. From across the bar, a man called out my name, walked over and introduced himself. With short dark hair and a neatly-trimmed beard, he introduced himself and said he went to my high school. A junior at college, Eric told me how freeing it was to be away from our hometown. I welcomed the chance to commiserate with him. The Cars' "Just What I Needed" played in the background.

"Finally," he said, "I can be out and proud!"

The first openly gay person I ever met, Eric told me he knew of my brother and a few of my brother's friends.

On the campus quad, lesbians in motorcycle jackets and spiky hair walked hand in hand. I envied them. They scared me.

Now in class we talked about ACT UP, how artists created change through action, in an era I watched from the sidelines, when I lived in Manhattan's East Village. I embarked on my first lesbian relationship at a time when gay bashing was a common occurrence. One student asked if I was involved with activist organizations. "I was closeted," I said. "Too scared to come out. I attended a couple of ACT UP meetings and felt the sizzling energy in the room, and cheered from the sidelines at ACT UP protests and gay pride parades." I also mentioned that I volunteered as a "buddy" to people with AIDS through the Gay Men's Health Crisis. Although the closet felt safer, it was stifling, as if gasping for breath, playing a role I hated, similar to the mute girl I performed while growing up.

At times I took part in the action, as long as I was anonymous, like the summer after I graduated college. With an organized group, I spray-painted stenciled shadows of briefcases on Wall Street to commemorate the Hiroshima bombings. I continued to attend marches and rallies for social justice.

Always more comfortable as an observer, except when I was in the spotlight, as if it were the sun. As an eight-year-old at summer camp, I belted out a song at a talent show. My father said he didn't recognize me. As an adult, after taking part in literary readings, acquaintances have said: "I didn't know you were funny, you seem so serious."

But out of the spotlight, I mostly revert back to Reserved Girl, like when I met with a film professor during my senior year of college. I had signed up for his performance art class, but the course didn't appear on my schedule. I thought there must have been a mistake, so I made my way to his office. Just back from a summer traveling on my own in Europe, of bargaining with men in the Turkish Bazaar and the Jerusalem's Old City Market, of pretending I didn't speak English and getting everything I bargained for, of taking busses and planes and trains alone at nineteen, and having the confidence and naivety to do it.

The moon-faced, balding man in black horn-rimmed glasses sat at his desk and stretched his arms behind his back.

"I signed up for your performance art class," I said, "but it's not on my schedule."

He stared at me. I suspect he'd already made up his mind: *Too boring*. "Do you want to tell me something about yourself?"

A poster of Alfred Hitchcock's profile stared me down. I had no idea I had to get approval to take the course. "I lived on a kibbutz this summer and traveled to Greece and Turkey, and I'm a photo major—"

"—Thank you," he said, and looked at the door.

And now I could ask of that film professor: Were you scared of what might have been unearthed if you set me free to create? Or did you think women had nothing to say? Instead you let in the drunken artist guys who stunk of body odor, and the stoned-out English majors who quoted Bukowski, all of whom seemed to create the same performance piece: In their goggles, they screamed while wielding an ax to a television set.

As professor of my first year seminar, I didn't require an interview. Anyone could sign up. We learned the value of process and possibility, the importance of creative expression. Now the spotlight on me felt ever more present; I hoped to model confidence but also reveal how I had "straight-washed" myself. Over the years, I've embraced my identity, and if I could do it, so could they.

On a regular basis, historians have "straight-washed" queer history, even in current times. My students watched the 2017 documentary about James Baldwin, *I am Not Your Negro*. I asked if they thought the director intentionally left out Baldwin's homosexuality. A student responded, "Baldwin dealt with being both Black and queer, and this was a focus of many of his novels and writings. Frankly, I find it incredibly disrespectful to act as if Baldwin was not a queer icon and activist."

My students knew of Keith Haring's drawings and murals but didn't know he was gay and died of AIDS. They knew of Emily Dickinson but had no idea she wrote hundreds of letters to Susan

Gilbert. Biographers believe Gilbert was the love of her life (and wife of Dickinson's brother, Austin). There is evidence that editors erased Susan's name, deleted lines, and changed pronouns from "she" to "he"; the letters that Susan wrote back to Emily were destroyed. In one letter, Emily wrote to Susan: "Never mind the letter, Susie; you have so much to do; just write me every week *one* line, and let it be, 'Emily, I love you,' and I will be satisfied!"

It's clear Dickinson's poetry served as a private release valve; most historians agree she wasn't interested in publishing. In fact, she wanted her manuscripts destroyed after her death. But her sister Lavinia asked Austin Dickinson's longtime mistress, Mabel Loomis Todd, to help her. Susan Gilbert and her descendants despised Todd.

After discussing the in-your-face actions of ACT UP and Grand Fury, students watched a short video about the AIDS Memorial Quilt, a project started with the intention of bringing in families to accept their relatives with AIDS, which it did. Some AIDS activists thought the quilt was too soft, not angry enough. But as a student pointed out, art provides a path to empathy.

I finally found it for myself in D.C. during the 1993 March on Washington for Lesbian, Gay, and Bi Equal Rights and Liberation, one of the largest protests in American history. I strolled near the Washington Monument, where hundreds of AIDS Quilt panels were on display, made by family and friends of those who succumbed to AIDS, in contrast to the many families who rejected their dying children and siblings. I read the panels and cried. Angered that the government didn't do more to find a cure; angered at myself for shutting off the valve to my heart. One panel in particular stuck with me:

"MY NAME IS DUANE KEARNS PURYEAR.

I WAS BORN ON DECEMBER 20, 1964.

I WAS DIAGNOSED WITH AIDS ON SEPTEMBER 7, 1987 AT 4:45 PM.

I WAS 22 YEARS OLD.
SOMETIMES, IT MAKES ME VERY SAD.
I MADE THIS PANEL MYSELF.
IF YOU ARE READING IT, I AM DEAD."

Two months into the semester, I arranged for an optional in-person hike with my students. I felt nervous, as if I were just about to meet an online date after Skyping for two months. *What should I wear? Would I be the confident professor in person, or revert back to the reserved girl?* At least I'd have my dog as a buffer. I arrived at the meeting spot and finally a gaggle of students in masks walked towards me. One I didn't recognize. On screen, she took up a lot of space, in a good way; in person, she was tiny, her mask taking up half her face. I let the others know I recognized them by looking their way and saying their names and quickly stepped into Confident Lori. Students jockeyed to walk by my side. They told me about their classes, their families, how they missed their pets. At the top of the mountain, we sat in a circle. Panda moved from student to student, licking their hands and faces, as if she sensed they all could use dog therapy. I asked them what they looked forward to. They said: going to parties, traveling, seeing their grandparents, not feeling anxious about their friends and family dying from COVID.

Before they returned to campus, I told them how anxious I was before meeting them, how it was like preparing for a face-to-face meeting with an internet date. "But," I said, "the date went well!"

We talked about how a number of contemporary artists have re-visioned queer history by painting and photo-shopping queer subject matter into dated settings. And then I showed my students a photo of my great aunt Irene, arm in arm with another woman, a big Chevy in the background. Aunt Irene, my grandmother's little sister, the only relative who cheered me on when I danced in my grandparents' apartment, who inspired me to explore the world, who never married. I told my students what it said on the back of the photo: *Daytona Beach, 1950,* but nothing more. "Tell me the story behind this picture," I said. "Reclaim history." One example that came out of this exercise:

Allison had recently moved to Florida where she was pursuing her dance career and decided to take a day to enjoy the beach. She looked to her right and was blessed with a gorgeous sight. Little did she know that would be her forever lover, Linda. Shortly before getting married, they decided to do a sort of "victory lap," taking pictures at each milestone of their relationship. Linda suggested that there was no better place to start than the beginning, and they quickly returned to the scene of their first meeting: Daytona Beach.

After students read their revised histories, I revealed the truth about the photo: "That's my great aunt Irene. She never got married and traveled the world." Students giggled; they also had aunts or uncles who have a "roommate" but never married.

Although this was not a hands-on art class, for their final projects, I required students to create a piece of art in any medium, inspired by at least two of the artists we've discussed. I let them know that they wouldn't be judged on the art itself, but the journey behind their process. On the last day of class, students presented their projects. One student said, "…my paintings speak deeply to my story thus far in figuring out my queer identity and my place in this world, and I'm proud of myself for being able to be that vulnerable in a classroom setting." Another said of the drawing she made, "It's almost an homage to how my own identity changed and developed throughout this course, through the material we learned about…Making it helped me examine my inner ongoing identity crisis…and my own personal queer experience in general."

There was so much love in that room that my heart almost leapt from my chest. Across the board, students loved the challenge of making a piece of art. "After this class," a student said, "I feel inspired and excited about my own art again."

I asked the class if they had any final thoughts. "I'm in tears," a student said, "after seeing everyone's projects. I'm a baby gay, and this class helped me so much. I never felt like I had a tribe before." Another said, "This class helped me unpack my identity. Because of it, I came out to my sister." Another student talked about making art in high school, but in the last few months, because of depression and COVID, hadn't made art all year. "But," she said, "I feel accomplished and inspired after making and presenting this project." And a final comment by a student: "This past semester was hard. I felt so isolated. But in this class I felt a sense of community; it made me feel really loved."

"Teaching this class," I said, "has helped clear away old bones in my closet." I showed them my Silence=Death T-shirt I bought from an ACT UP booth at a West Village street festival in 1988, still in perfect condition; I only wore it once to an 80's dance party.

I continue to release my own valves, to embrace my queerness, of sloughing off the pain of hiding in the closet, of discarding the protective shell of who I thought I needed to be, of the shame that told me I'm not good enough for friendship or love, so I should grasp onto crumbs and put up with cheaters and liars and alcoholics because that's all I deserved. A door I kept knocking on but a door that was only a mirror to my own closed down heart.

Now I could say I'm on the frontlines, cheering my students on, the same way Aunt Irene cheered me on when I danced in my grandparents' Brighton Beach apartment, of giving students the support and confidence I never had, as we reclaim our lives, and our history, together.

UNLIMITED MINUTES

1

I WRITE THIS ON MOTHER'S DAY during the pandemic, thirty-three years after I last spent time with my mother, when I sat next to her on the steps of my childhood home and flipped through photos she had taken in Portugal with a 110 instamatic camera, her last trip abroad. Beaches and cathedrals and mules strolling through narrow streets. I had sublet my Manhattan apartment and bought a discount ticket to Frankfurt, with plans to travel in Europe for two months. Three weeks after touching down in Germany, I woke up from a nightmare of a car burning and free-wrote in my journal, letting my unconscious dictate: *You need to come home. Please come on home.* I scribbled this over and over. I later learned that as I wrote, my mother took her last breath.

2

TWO MONTHS BEFORE MOTHER'S DAY OF 2020, I had been sleeping at a beachfront hotel in Sagres, Portugal, when a string of text messages lit up my phone: *You need to come home.* President Trump announced U.S. borders will close to incoming international travelers in *two days time*. I woke my girlfriend up. We already had a ticket home in less than 48 hours. She went back to bed. Covid-19 had crept up on us.

Our flight to Portugal had originated in New York City. Crowds of people still scurried down Broadway, taxis still honked, restaurants still bustled. I boarded a commuter train to visit my father and stepmother on Long Island. As usual, I brought bagels, whitefish salad and a jar of pickled herring. He loved the herring but said I was crazy for traveling. And besides, he added, "There's nothing to see in Portugal." I told him we had prepared: we brought hand sanitizer, gloves, and bandanas. Although the virus had affected Italy and parts of Spain, we hadn't cancelled our trip, as there were no known cases in Portugal.

Once there, we toured a cork forest, drank acorn brandy, strolled through multi-colored castles, walked on the beach and took pictures of a monolithic lighthouse. We relaxed. Until receiving the text messages.

The Lisbon Airport and our flight back to New York were jam-packed. On the plane, an off-duty Brazilian flight attendant sat next to me. He said he didn't worry about catching the virus—as long as he took the proper precautions he'd be fine. In New York, the customs agent asked if I traveled anywhere other than Portugal, then stamped my passport. While we waited for a flight to North Carolina, our server at Ruby Tuesdays said, "It's only a matter of time before the airports shuts down." A single mother without savings, she feared for her livelihood. We made it back to Asheville just before midnight, and a friend picked us up from the airport. We wore gloves and bandanas on our faces.

My father had left two voicemail messages, asking if I had the virus. The next day I told him I was glad I had the chance to see him; no way I could have seen him after the trip and now I had to quarantine myself for two weeks. I told him my school gave us an extra week of spring break to prepare for teaching online. To distract him, I sent a picture of my German shepherd mix, Panda. "She's a beautiful animal," he said. "She could be a dog model."

3

WHEN I MET MY CREATIVE NONFICTION WORKSHOP on Zoom, I checked in with each student. They said they were glad to be back in class and have some semblance of normalcy. One student moved home into her parents' trailer. She leaned in and said it wasn't easy. In the past, this student told me her mother drank a lot and listened nonstop to Def Leppard.

Before spring break, I started each class with a free-writing exercise, and I continued this routine. But now I gave them "pandemic prompts," such as, "What I've learned about myself because of social isolation is..." They began with the prompt and continued to write whatever came to their minds for six minutes. If they chose to, they read their passages aloud. Most did. They were troopers and shared vulnerable words about fears and hopes. On the last day of class, I gave them a final prompt: "In five years, what I'll remember about the quarantine is..." As they read, I jotted down their future memories: "Laughing at the tree that creaked and swayed and wondering if the roots had snapped," "Not getting enough sleep and regretting it," "The bare shelves in the supermarket and thinking of my grandmother who grew up in the Depression," and "How clean the house was and whether I'll touch my grandmother's hands again."

Today I think about what I'd remember in five years: that I was the age of my mother when she lost her life; that my hair grew longer and grayer than it had been in a long time; that I'd never seen my mother's hair gray, only different shades of red; that despite the quarantine, I managed to meet, over Zoom, with three writing groups on a regular basis; that I created a music prompt group with four musician friends. Once a week we met to share a song we had written, inspired by a prompt we had agreed on the week before. I hadn't written music in years, not since the early 90's when I was in an all-girls rock band, Rapunzel, but now I loved the challenge of it, of hearing what the others had come up with.

In five years, I'll remember that during the quarantine, I bought a new guitar, and taught Kristen basic chords on my old guitar, a guitar I had bought for ninety-nine dollars when, at fifteen years old, I first learned to play.

And I thought about my mother, who, like me, had been active with different communities—she had taken lead roles in two Jewish women's organizations, and during a benefit auction, she bid five dollars for five guitar lessons. My father dropped me off at a guitar studio and a clean-cut guy who wore a gold Italian horn around his neck taught me the chords to the Eagles' "Take it Easy," and Peter Frampton's "Show Me the Way." He assigned pages and pages of exercises from a Mel Bay beginning guitar book. When I played in front of him, I'd get anxious and mess up. "Are you sure you practiced?" he asked.

After five lessons, I'd had it with Mel Bay and the guitar teacher. I'm not sure where my mother found another teacher—a skinny blonde hippie with long fingernails and John Lennon glasses. In my hot-pink bedroom, he taught me to finger pick and play Spanish guitar. During the fifth lesson, he asked if I had a boyfriend. I said no. He said, "Do you want one?" I shrugged and I'm sure my face turned red and we continued. He might have been twenty. I don't remember telling my mother about his question, but I'm pretty sure the lessons ended. I still can play a mean "Magdalena."

In five years I'll remember organizing Zoom reunions with college friends, some of whom I hadn't seen since graduation. During one meeting, a friend spoke about her father, who died the week before. He had been in the hospital for a heart condition but Covid took him out. Another said her mother had just been diagnosed with stage 4 lung cancer. Another, whose father lay on a couch nearby, said, "He's got dementia and Parkinson's Disease."

During one reunion, a friend mentioned our trips out west, how the two of us hitchhiked up and down the Pacific Coast. This was during the Ted Bundy days, but at the time, I didn't know about Bundy and vaguely heard about women hitchhikers getting their arms chopped off. But that didn't deter us. Never once did we feel threatened. And only once did I think about whether my mother had worried about me. A businessman picked us up and bought us lunch. At a restaurant overlooking the Pacific, he asked if our parents had any idea we were hitchhiking. He said, "What if they knew? Would they be concerned?"

At the time, sadly, I didn't think they'd care. When I had shown my mother pictures from my travels, or told her stories about new friends I had met on the road, she'd be humming, or vaguely listening.

All I knew for sure was that time was limitless and I was invincible. But now I know better.

Before her death, my mother might have lost her spirit— the spirit I'd heard about from her cousin and college friend, a spirit that moved her to create art, to laugh and joke. Only able to demonstrate love and affection to our black poodle, how could she be concerned about her youngest daughter holding her thumb out on Highway One, smiling and waving to truckers and men in souped-up Camaros? Maybe she'd think, *free is always a good deal*. After all, when an anarchist friend gave me a list of calling card numbers belonging to big corporations, numbers I could tap into public phones and make free calls, my mother asked for one and used it from the house, even though I warned her against that. Operators later asked if she knew anyone who used a credit card number from her phone. She told them that her children had all kinds of friends stay over.

In five years, I'll remember I called my father often. And he called me too. He said, "If I were in one of those nursing homes, I'd already be dead." I'll remember that at almost 93, he was sharp as a tack, mostly, but struggled with Parkinson's Disease and was confined to a wheelchair. Yet every now and then paranoia kicked in and he claimed his aide had been trying to kill him.

I'll remember that I walked every day in the woods with Kristen and our three dogs, how one of her dogs—a shepherd/greyhound mix named Noodles, tucked her tail between her legs as soon as she spotted a stranger, but when I sang a song consisting only of her name repeated over and over, she stopped in her tracks, smiled and jumped up, as if to say, "That's my song!" I'll remember how I slept better than I had slept in a long while, and how, for the first time in my adult life, I felt secure with myself, my relationship, and had a sense of family. I'll remember how Kristen and I cooked dinner, cuddled up on my futon and watched the new *L-Word: Generation Q.* How we agreed that the show's gratuitous drama was over the top but also agreed that we'd rather get our fix from the show than in our lives, that the most consistent drama we experienced was watching our dogs raise their hackles and growl, attempting, sometimes with success, to steal bones from each other. I'll also remember that a minute or two later, they'd work it out and chew their bones, content to be lying side by side.

4

ONE STUDENT SAID WHAT HE'LL REMEMBER about the quarantine is how he never thought he'd move back home, but in five years he'd remember how he took the time to get to know his younger sisters, how his whole family took the time to love one another.

While he talked, I thought about how I'd feel if I had to move home while in college, how I'd probably have raided the liquor cabinet to cope with anxiety. Even though I never drank much, when I went home for a few days during holidays, I often cracked open the apricot brandy bottle or vodka and took a swig.

Envious of my student and his loving family, I thought about a question a therapist I had seen asked me a decade ago. At each session, she said, "Imagine if you had the perfect parents, the perfect mother, what would your life look like?"

I sighed loudly and said, "Who decides what's perfect?" I stared at the therapist's drooping white socks, and overheard another therapist in the next room, mixed with white noise. "I didn't have the perfect parents so I can't imagine that."

Eventually, I said something like, "Maybe the perfect parents would have encouraged me; maybe they would have asked about my writing, my art, what I learned in school. Maybe they'd worry and ask me to call home." What I didn't say was I had to "grow myself up," a phrase a friend used after she met my parents. Perhaps my absent parents made me more resilient, always in search of creative outlets so that I'd have to nourish myself.

Maybe "perfect parent," is a vague concept, like God.

If I had parents who nourished me, maybe it wouldn't have taken until my mid-fifties to figure out what a healthy relationship should look like. Maybe I'd feel more confident and be further along in my artistic career. Or maybe I'd feel entitled, or wouldn't have found the courage to travel and take as many risks, or perhaps, because I saw my mother confined, I took it upon myself to do everything she couldn't.

5

ON MOTHER'S DAY DURING THE PANDEMIC, I call my stepmother. She's frail, uses a cane, and is hard of hearing. When I last saw her, she had attempted to slice a bagel but it fell on the floor. Now she tells me she took her hearing aids out. "You're calling," she says, "to wish me a Happy Mother's Day? Thank you." Click.

Three months after my mother's death, my father had met his future wife on a blind date arranged by his accountant. Grateful he found someone to endure his non-stop chatter and obsessions, I wondered how she found the patience. Maybe zoning out, ignoring him, like my mother did, was her way to cope.

At times I feel my mother's presence, that maybe she's watching out for me. Or maybe I need to believe this to feel okay about the mother I never knew. It lets me imagine that if she were alive today, she'd be a feisty ninety-year-old. And now with unlimited minutes, she'd be in touch often. After retiring from teaching kindergarten in Queens, she'd pick up a sketchpad and paintbrush and create art again. And take up gardening.

So today, I imagine I call my mother on Zoom. She shows me red geraniums hanging in macramé plant holders, woven by her years before. She has on blue eye shadow, lipstick and the same uneven face foundation that never quite blended into her neck. She holds up a small watercolor painting of the geranium, the strokes a little shaky, the background her favorite color, turquoise. "Something to do," she says in her thick Brooklyn accent.

I tell her I love it, that the contrast between the colors makes it vibrate. My dog steps up onto my chair, licks my face and takes up half of my image.

"Hello Panda!" she says.

I pick up my laptop and carry it out to my yard, where azaleas, peonies, and irises bloomed, that much of the florae planted over the last couple years reappeared, to my surprise, resistant against persistent voles. Even the sage, oregano and ferns sprouted back to life. "Almost a miracle," I say. "Just two weeks ago, I wrote them off for dead."

She nods, leans into the camera to get a better look. "They're thriving," she says, "because you took good care of them." Her wild gray hair explodes in all directions. "You gave them love. They're giving it back."

LORI HORVITZ is the author of the memoir-essay collection, *The Girls of Usually*, winner of the USA Best Book Award in Gay & Lesbian Nonfiction, and Gold Medal Winner IPPY BOOK AWARD in Autobiography/ Memoir. Her creative nonfiction has appeared in a variety of journals and anthologies including *Under the Sun, Hobart, Epiphany, South Dakota Review, Redivider, Chattahoochee Review, The Guardian, Bustle,* and *Hotel Amerika*. She has been awarded writing fellowships from The Ragdale Foundation, Brush Creek, Yaddo, Cottages at Hedgebrook, Virginia Center for the Creative Arts, and Blue Mountain Center. Professor of English at UNC Asheville, Horvitz received a Ph.D. in English from SUNY at Albany, and an MFA in Creative Writing from Brooklyn College. She lives in Asheville, North Carolina.

Manufactured by Amazon.ca
Bolton, ON

32043271R00132